"At the moment I'm between women."

Steve put out his cigarette and drained his glass of wine. His eyes held Loren's mockingly.

"I refuse to act as a diversion," she said stiffly.

"I don't consider you a diversion, Loren. I consider you a challenge. A raw country girl who's never gone to bed with a man...yes, quite a challenge."

"Is this your subtle way of telling me that at some time in the future you intend persuading me into your bed?"

"Does the thought excite you?"

"To be quite frank, it amuses me."

He paused in the process of refilling their glasses. "May I ask why you find it amusing?"

"Well, it's either that or slapping your face." She glanced around the crowded restaurant. "Which would you prefer?"

Books by Yvonne Whittal

HARLEQUIN ROMANCES

HARLEQUIN PRESENTS

These books may be available at your local bookseller.

For a free catalog listing all titles currently available, send your name and address to:

Harlequin Reader Service
P.O. Box 52040, Phoenix, AZ 85072-2040
Canadian address: Stratford, Ontario N5A 6W2

Ride the Wind

Yvonne Whittal

Harlequin Books

TORONTO • NEW YORK • LONDON
AMSTERDAM • PARIS • SYDNEY • HAMBURG
STOCKHOLM • ATHENS • TOKYO • MILAN

Original hardcover edition published in 1983
by Mills & Boon Limited

ISBN 0-373-02616-1

Harlequin Romance first edition April 1984

CHAPTER ONE

THE steel blades of the windmill turned slowly in the reluctant breeze that drifted across the parched Karoo veld, and it pumped a weak stream of water into the corrugated tank which had never once been filled to capacity during that long, hot summer. The drought had been severe, killing off much of the vegetation required for the sheep, and Loren Fraser screwed up her tawny eyes in the blazing sun as she stared at the fleecy clouds hovering over the distant hills.

'There's no rain there,' her father remarked, guessing her thoughts as he followed the direction of her gaze.

'You're right,' she sighed despondently, turning towards the tall, rugged-faced man beside her. 'It's too late in the season for rain.'

'Perhaps we'll have good rains after the coming winter,' Will Fraser echoed the hopes of most of the Karoo farmers in the district.

His face and arms had been burnt a deep ochre in the sun, and beneath the wide brim of the sweat-stained hat his dark eyes mirrored that same look of mingled hope and despair which she had seen in the eyes of so many of the sheep farmers in the Aberdeen area that summer. They would never give up hoping, but they were beginning to know once again the meaning of despair.

'We have to take the bad years with the good years, and this drought can't last for ever,' Will voiced the tough rule by which they had had to live most of their lives.

Loren smiled wanly as she listened to the mournful squeak of the windmill, and turned her head once again to gaze out across the arid veld where the sheep still attempted to graze in the camp beyond the fence.

'What's on your mind, Loren?' her father's gravelly voice intruded on her thoughts. 'You look as if you're carrying the problems of the world on your shoulders!'

She pushed the tips of her fingers into the pockets of her denims and stared contemplatively down at her dusty boots. This was the opening she had waited for, but now she needed every scrap of courage to do what she knew she could no longer delay.

'I'm leaving my job with Mr Kruger,' she plunged in at the deep end, and her words seemed to hover between them in the brief but strained silence that followed.

'You've resigned?'

'I resigned at the beginning of the month, and I finish up this coming Thursday.'

There were no recriminations, which was typical of her father, but his next query was like dumping a wildcat amongst the farm chickens. 'Does your mother know?'

'I haven't told her yet,' Loren confessed, catching her lip between small, perfect teeth. 'I was hoping I could depend on your support when I tell her this evening.'

Will Fraser's hand fumbled towards his pipe in the top pocket of his sweat-stained khaki shirt, but he relinquished the idea of stoking up, and let his hand fall to his side again. 'It isn't going to be easy convincing your mother that you've done the right thing.'

'I know,' Loren grimaced. 'Dad, I'm so tired of all the attempts at matchmaking that have been going on these past few years. What no one seems to understand is that I'm not ready for marriage, and I refuse to be pushed into something I don't want.'

'Have you decided where you're going?'

'Yes.' She frowned down at her dusty boots as if her

inspiration came from there. 'I'm going to Johannesburg.'

The windmill squeaked and groaned into the afternoon silence as if pumping water from the bowels of the earth had become an effort instead of a joy, and Loren felt the strain as if it were her own.

'Johannesburg is a long way away from here, but if that's what you want . . .'

Will Fraser left his sentence unfinished, but there was no need to say more, and he placed a heavy arm about Loren's shoulders as they walked slowly across the parched, dusty earth to where he had parked his truck.

Her father had been right about it not being easy to convince her mother that she had made the right decision, but now she at least had someone on her side, and that Sunday evening, after dinner, she broke the news of her intended departure to her mother.

'You've *resigned*?' Jean Fraser's voice was shrill with shock and agitation as she dropped her table napkin on to the table next to her coffee cup. 'So that post Matt Kruger's been advertising is not for someone to assist you?'

'It's for someone to replace me,' Loren confirmed, looking directly into tawny eyes so very like her own, and she saw the confusion there which her announcement had aroused.

'But why? Matt Kruger's such a——'

'I know, Mother,' Loren cut in impatiently. 'He's such a good attorney and such a nice man, but you know as well as I do that lately everyone in the district has been speculating about our relationship.'

'It's only natural,' Jean Fraser protested. 'You've been working for him a long time, and he's taken you out quite a few times.'

'And on that flimsy basis everyone has predicted that

it won't be long before they hear wedding bells ringing in Aberdeen,' Loren concluded cynically.

'You're no longer a child, Loren, you're twenty-five.'

'Exactly!' Loren quelled her rising anger and forced herself to remain calm. 'Mother, please try to understand. I appreciate the fact that everyone is so concerned about my unmarried status, but it's become annoying and embarrassing for me as well as the men who have risked being seen with me.'

'Matt Kruger hasn't been angered or embarrassed by it,' her mother argued, and Loren sighed inwardly.

'Matt Kruger is a dear, sweet man, and one day he'll make some lucky woman a wonderful husband, but I don't intend to be that woman.'

Jean Fraser sighed, the hint of grey at her temples adding to her attractiveness. 'Sometimes I think you simply don't want to get married.'

'That's not true, and you know it, Mother. I think every woman wants a husband and children, but——'

'But the right man hasn't come along yet,' Will Fraser intervened for the first time.

'The right man!' Jean snorted disparagingly. 'The problem with Loren is she never lets any man get close enough to her to find out whether he might be the right man or not.'

'And who does she take after in that respect?' Will argued, a teasing smile lighting up his dark eyes as he looked at his wife. 'You were twenty-eight when I met you, and until then you'd never let any man get close to you, but I came along and swept you off your feet.'

'You never swept me off my feet,' Jean protested indignantly.

'I came pretty close to it, when you think we knew each other only two months before we were married.'

'I admit that, but——' Loren saw her mother falter and gesture helplessly with her hands. 'Don't think for one moment that I was cool and unaffected by what was going on around me. My friends were getting married and having children. I was happy for them, and I envied them, but I wasn't simply going to marry the first man who might come along. If you hadn't stormed into my life, Will, I would have been sitting on the shelf, and I dread the thought of that happening to Loren.'

Her anxious eyes met Loren's, and Loren reached across the table to grip her mother's hand. 'I love you, Mother, and I appreciate your concern, but you must realise that the situation here in Aberdeen has become intolerable for me.'

'Where will you go?' Jean asked resignedly.

'I've found myself a job in Johannesburg with a company called Beaumont Engineering, and I start there next week Monday.'

'Why Johannesburg, of all places?' her mother protested.

'They offered the best salary for my qualifications.'

'And where will you stay?'

'I'll find accommodation in a hotel first of all, but it will give me time to look for a suitable flat somewhere.'

During the ensuing silence Jean Fraser glanced at her husband as if she were silently seeking advice, then she sighed audibly and a sad smile curved her mouth. 'Well, if that's what you want, then I suppose there's nothing your father and I can do about it.'

On the eve of her departure Loren stood on the verandah of her parents' home. She felt sad. It had been a day of saying farewell to the people and the things she knew, and none of it had been pleasant. Matt Kruger had been a good employer and a good friend, but they had been thrown together too often by the Aberdeen matchmakers, and their speculations had finally become too embarrassing for Loren to bear.

The most difficult part was yet to come. She would have to take her leave of her parents and this semi-desert part of the country which she loved so much, and it was not something she was looking forward to. She lifted her gaze to the ink-black sky where the stars glittered so brightly one had the feeling you could reach out and touch them. Nowhere else could one see the stars quite like this, and nowhere else could the air smell sweeter than after the first summer rains which had been so elusive this past year. In the distance a jackal howled at the moon as if he too felt the effect of the drought, and Loren sighed as she entered the silent house and went to her room.

She ought to be in bed and asleep if she wanted to make an early start the following morning, but she was feeling much too restless. The wardrobe mirror reflected the image of a tall, slender young woman with glossy, honey-gold hair waving naturally on to her shoulders, but Loren seldom paused long enough in front of the mirror to admire herself. Her tawny eyes, an attractive mixture of brown and gold, looked troubled, and her long lashes cast shadows across her perfectly modelled cheekbones. Her nose was small and straight, and above the firmly rounded chin her mouth was sensitive and full with the promise of passion in the slight upward curve of the upper lip. She was attractive, and there was an aura of aloofness hovering about her which most men found intriguing, but none of them had been given the opportunity to get close enough to find out what lay beneath that cool exterior. No one, that was, except Matt Kruger.

Matt! Loren thought of him now as she sat down on her bed and stared at her suitcases standing packed and ready for her departure in the morning. Matt Kruger could be a ruthless attorney, but as a man he was kind and considerate. After four years as his private secretary a bond of friendship had developed between them which had allowed for a deeper understanding of each other, and Matt had been the first to sense that she was finding it a strain coping with the pressure brought to bear on her.

'You ought to get right away from here,' he had suggested one morning. 'You're a secretary in a million, and I don't want to lose you, but I'm making this suggestion for your own good.'

A smile lifted the corners of Loren's mouth when she recalled how shocked she had been at the time. The thought of leaving the plains of the Karoo had been abhorrent to her, but as time went by she had begun to see the sense of it. She had to go where her personal life was no one's concern but her own, and that was when she had started seeking employment elsewhere in earnest. Beaumont Engineering in Johannesburg had made her the most incredible offer, and she had flown up from George one Friday morning for an interview. Her application had been accepted, the necessary documents had been completed, and she had flown back that same day without anyone other than Matt Kruger knowing the true reason for the excursion.

Loren stifled a yawn and glanced at the bedside clock. Twelve-thirty! She would have to get some sleep if she was to leave early in the morning, and heaven only knew where she would find herself the following night.

She slept very badly, her dreams a chaotic blend of the past and the unknown future, but somehow she awoke feeling refreshed the following morning. Her parents had agreed that there would be no sad, prolonged farewells, but that did not prevent Loren from feeling choked when she finally drove away from the farm in her green Stanza on that April morning. She had many hours of travelling ahead of her, and it looked as if it was going to be another scorchingly hot day with barely a cloud in the sky.

It was a long, tiring journey, but Loren made several stops along the way and, as a result, it was early evening before she booked herself into a hotel in Johannesburg. She soaked her weary body in a hot bath and changed into something suitable for dinner, but she booked a call to her parents before she went down.

'I've been so worried about you doing this long trip on your own!' her mother's voice wailed across the crackling connection when Loren eventually got through to them.

'I'm perfectly well, Mother,' Loren assured her. 'I'm a bit tired at the moment, but a good night's sleep will cure that.'

'I hope you're staying in a respectable hotel?'

Loren cast a swift glance about the room, taking in her luxurious surroundings for the first time, and smiled wryly. 'It's very respectable.'

'Write to us and let us know if you need anything,' her father said moments later when he had the opportunity to speak to her.

'I'll write as soon as I'm settled,' Loren promised, and she felt a little lost some minutes later when she replaced the receiver which severed the link with the familiarity of her home.

She stared at her suitcases, but there was no time now to unpack them. It was eight-thirty, and the hotel's *à la carte* restaurant beckoned invitingly when she felt the first pangs of hunger.

The restaurant was reasonably full, Loren noticed when she was shown to her table. Basket-woven shades concealed the lights which hung low over the tables, and the silver gleamed on wine-red tablecloths. She placed her order, and poured herself a glass of water from the carafe while she waited. Her casual, disinterested gaze wandered across the room and settled finally on the two men seated at the table close to her own. It was obvious that the reason for this dinner engagement was business and not pleasure, and she watched their briefcases being flipped open from time to time to study and exchange documents. It was the one man in particular, however, who captured and held her attention. His hair was a dark mahogany brown, cut short and tapering neatly into his strong neck, and his shoulders looked wide and powerful beneath the superb cut of his dark grey jacket.

Loren paid little attention to the fillet steak which was eventually placed before her. Her glance was drawn repeatedly and irresistibly towards the two men who were so deeply involved in a discussion, and she nibbled absently at her food while she studied the strong profile of the younger man in the dark suit who sat with his back turned slightly towards her. His features were tanned as if he spent many hours in the sun, and her glance lingered with something close to pleasure on the broad forehead, high-bridged nose, and the perfectly chiselled mouth. He was good-looking in a rugged sort of way, and she liked what she saw. How old was he? Thirty-five? Forty, perhaps?

He turned his head completely as if he had sensed that he was being observed, and their eyes met for one electrifying second before she hastily lowered her gaze to concentrate on her food. Her face felt hot, and her heart was hammering so hard against her ribs that she felt certain he must hear it across the distance separating them.

Loren did not dare glance in his direction again, but she knew that, this time, she was the one who was being observed, and it was a most disconcerting experience to know that she was being assessed. During that brief moment when their eyes had met she had felt a certain animal magnetism emanating from him, and little shivers were coursing their way up and down her spine as she felt rather than saw his eyes roaming over her.

A movement finally made her glance up to see him preparing to leave the restaurant with his elderly companion, and their eyes met again for one brief second. She felt the impact of his glance like a shock penetrating her to the marrow, and she sighed with relief when he was gone.

Only then could she give her complete attention to the tastefully prepared fillet steak in front of her, but when she eventually went up to her room she found that she could not entirely forget the man she had seen in the restaurant. There had been something too vital and too dynamic about him to make him easy to forget, but it was unlikely that she would ever see him again, and that was perhaps just as well.

Loren spent the weekend driving around to become acquainted with the city, and on the Monday morning she reported for duty at eight-thirty precisely. The temporary pass she had been issued with saw her through Beaumont Engineering's security gate, and the Accounts department was not difficult to find on the ground floor of the steel and concrete building which housed the offices. Harvey Griffin, the Chief Accountant, was a short, stout little man with dark-rimmed glasses and a friendly manner and, from the orderly state of the office she would have to work in, she gathered that his previous secretary had been a meticulous worker. Everything was where it ought to be, and this made settling down in her new post considerably easier for Loren.

Harvey Griffin had told her that they served an excellent lunch in the staff canteen, and when Loren left her office shortly after one o'clock that day she found

herself confronted by a pretty brunette emerging from
the office across the passage.

'You're Loren Fraser, Mr Griffin's new secretary,
aren't you?' she asked as she fell into step beside Loren.

'That's correct.'

'I'm Natalie Miller, and I also work in Accounts,' she
introduced herself, then her dark eyes gazed question-
ingly at Loren. 'I'm on my way to the canteen, if you'd
like me to show you the way?'

'Thank you,' Loren smiled with relief at not having
to wander around aimlessly in this vast building before
finding what she was looking for.

The canteen was filled almost to capacity, but they
helped themselves to a cold lunch and found a vacant
table at the opposite end of the enormous room.

'Have you been working here long?' Loren asked
conversationally over lunch.

'Almost four years.'

'I imagine you know most of the people working here.'

'I'll say I do,' Natalie Miller laughed, her eyes
crinkling attractively at the corners, then she sobered
and studied Loren closely. 'You worked for an
attorney, didn't you?'

'Yes,' Loren replied, somewhat surprised that Natalie
Miller should know so much about her. 'It feels a bit
strange finding myself an employee of such a vast
organisation.'

'You'll get used to it,' Natalie said confidently,
polishing off her lunch and pouring their tea. 'Where
are you staying?'

'I have a room in a hotel at the moment, but I'm
hoping to get a flat somewhere soon.'

'Flats aren't that easy to find here in Johannesburg if
you're looking for one in a respectable area that doesn't
cost the earth,' Natalie dampened Loren's hopes. 'Are
you in a hurry to find a place of your own?'

'I am rather,' Loren admitted with a wry smile. 'It's a bit expensive living in a hotel.'

Natalie put down her cup and studied Loren thoughtfully. 'My sister and brother-in-law are looking for someone to stay in their flat for three months while they're in Europe The rental they want is very low, and it will give you more time to find something else.'

'Well, I . . . I don't know,' Loren floundered, almost speechless at the unexpected offer.

'Look, I'll give you their address and I'll meet you there this evening at seven-thirty. You can look the place over and decide whether you would like to stay,' Natalie forestalled Loren's refusal and, whipping a pen out of her skirt pocket, she scribbled down the address on the reverse side of their lunch docket.

'I don't quite know what to say,' Loren shook her head as Natalie pushed the slip of paper across the table towards her. 'You don't even know me.'

'I'm a pretty good judge of character, you have to be in this city if you want to survive,' she announced gravely, then she tapped the slip of paper with her forefinger. 'I'd like you to meet my sister and to see the place. You can decide afterwards what to do about accepting or rejecting the offer.'

'You're very kind.'

'Think nothing of it,' Natalie brushed aside the matter airily, and Loren felt quite overwhelmed when they left the canteen some minutes later.

Harvey Griffin was not an exacting boss, and Loren did no more than feel her way around on that first day at Beaumont Engineering. At her hotel that evening she had an early dinner and, after asking a few directions from the desk clerk in the foyer, she drove to the address Natalie Miller had given her.

Fifteen minutes later she was parking her Stanza outside in a grey brick building which was reasonably modern, and had a neat outward appearance, but now that she was there she felt nervous about the whole idea of even contemplating moving into someone else's flat. Not wanting to let Natalie down, she took the lift up to the ninth floor, and at precisely seven-thirty she rang the bell outside the wood-panelled door.

Natalie Miller, looking much younger in jeans and a sweater, opened the door for her and swept her inside to meet her sister, Caroline, and her brother-in-law, Robert York. There was very little likeness between the two sisters. Caroline was as fair as Natalie was dark, but there was little time to actually get acquainted before Natalie and Caroline took her on a tour through the modern, expensively furnished flat with all the conveniences one could possibly dream of in a home. It was a one-bedroomed flat with a north-facing front to receive the full extent of the sun during the day, and everything in the flat would be at Loren's disposal if she chose to move in.

'Well, what do you think?' Natalie prodded her excitedly when they returned to the lounge and the glass of wine which Robert had poured for them in their absence.

'It's a beautiful flat, and very nicely situated,' Loren began hesitantly, not wanting to commit herself.

'You'll take it, then?' Caroline asked anxiously, then she laughed a little selfconsciously at her own hastiness, and explained, 'We're really rather desperate, you see. We're leaving the day after tomorrow, and we would like to know that there'll be someone staying here whom we could trust to take care of everything for us.'

Amusement lurked in Loren's tawny eyes. 'How do you know you can trust me?'

'If Natalie says you're okay, then that's good enough for us,' Caroline replied, and Robert York nodded his dark head to confirm this when Loren happened to glance in his direction.

There was no earthly reason why she should not accept this generous offer, Loren decided, and her smile broadened when she met Caroline and Natalie's anxious glances. 'I'll stay and look after everything for you.'

'Wonderful!' the two sisters exclaimed almost simultaneously, and, after the final details were discussed, Loren relaxed and spent a pleasant evening in their company before she returned to the hotel.

Loren's second day at Beaumont Engineering went much smoother than the first, and having Natalie for a friend helped to overcome the strangeness of her new environment. Natalie was a mine of information whenever she popped into Loren's office, and Loren found herself becoming acquainted with a number of the staff members before she had even met them.

They were on their way to the canteen that day when the lift doors slid open on the ground floor and a tall man strode out briskly with an elderly, trim-looking woman in tow. *It was him*! It was the man she had seen in the hotel restaurant on her first night in Johannesburg, and the shock of recognition was like several volts of electricity shooting through her.

'Get that contract in the post first thing in the morning, Mrs Markham,' he was saying in a deep-throated voice as his long strides took him swiftly towards the exit.

'Yes, sir,' said the woman at his side, and she was almost running to keep up with him.

'If there should be any queries, then you may refer them to Jim MacDonald.'

'Yes, sir,' the woman said again, following him out of the building, and moments later they were out of sight.

'Who was that?' Loren asked, expelling the air slowly from her lungs.

'That, my dear Loren, was the big chief himself,' Natalie informed her with an affected voice. 'I suppose one could call Steve Beaumont the captain of this vast ship we sail in daily, and not a move is made without him knowing about it.'

'Steve Beaumont,' Loren repeated his name almost without realising she had spoken while they continued to walk towards the canteen.

'You look as if you've seen a ghost.'

'*What*?' Loren came swiftly to her senses. 'Oh, I— he's really quite a striking man.'

'You can say that again!' Natalie laughed in reply to Loren's lame excuse for how she must have looked, and, when they entered the canteen and helped themselves to lunch, Natalie added in a lowered voice, 'There's not a female in this company who wouldn't give her false eyelashes for just five minutes alone with him, but he keeps very much to himself, and there's little anyone knows about his private life.'

The discussion on Steve Beaumont ended there, but Loren was left feeling vaguely uneasy for some reason she could not even explain to herself.

For the rest of that day, *and* the next, Loren felt nervous and jumpy and quite unlike herself. It had to be the excitement of moving into Caroline and Robert's flat, she convinced herself, and she felt a great deal better when Natalie popped her head round the door of her office late that afternoon.

'Do you need any help moving in this evening?'

'I haven't very much to move in with,' Loren laughed, 'but I wouldn't mind the company.'

'In that case I'll see you at the flat on my way back from the airport.'

Natalie was gone before Loren could reply, and half an hour later it was time to go home. *Home*. For the next three months home would be someone else's flat, and after that she hoped to be in a position to move into a place of her own.

Loren was in no hurry to leave the hotel that evening. She wanted to give Caroline and Robert time to leave for the airport before she moved in, so she changed into a comfortable pair of slacks and a warm sweater before she packed the remainder of her things. She had dinner sent up to her room and, after a leisurely meal, went downstairs to settle her bill and arrange for someone to collect her suitcases.

She was collecting the key from the caretaker of the flats shortly after eight that evening when Natalie arrived.

'I'll show you where to park your car in the basement, then I'll help you up with your suitcases,' she offered, following Loren out to where her Stanza was parked in the street.

With Natalie's help they had to make only one trip up to the ninth floor flat, and Loren was grateful for her company while she unpacked and became acquainted with everything.

'Did Caroline and Robert get away safely?' Loren asked when she had stashed away her empty suitcases.

'There were a few last-minute hassles, but the plane left on time,' Natalie replied, taking Loren's arm and almost dragging her towards the kitchen. 'Let me show you where everything is kept.'

The kitchen cupboards were far from empty, and the refrigerator was fully stocked with everything she could possibly require until she had time to go shopping for herself. They made coffee and talked late into the night, and by the time Natalie went home Loren felt quite at ease in her new surroundings.

Loren wrote a long letter home to her parents at the end of that week, hoping to set their minds at rest about her welfare, and she wrote a much briefer letter to Matt Kruger, who had insisted that she keep in touch. She missed him almost as much as she missed her parents, but she had little time to think about it during the following weeks while she came to grips with her job.

'Miss Fraser, would you please take these reports up to Mr MacDonald?' Harvey Griffin asked one afternoon, placing a loosely bound file of papers on her desk. 'You'll find his office on the fourth floor, room 403.'

'Certainly, Mr Griffin,' Loren replied, rising at once to carry out his instructions.

She had never been up to the fourth floor before, but she knew that the directors of the company had their offices up there. Natalie had mockingly called it 'hallowed ground', and Loren laughed softly to herself at the description as she thumbed the lift button.

The lights above the lift door indicated that it was descending to ground level, and Loren stepped forward automatically when the steel doors slid open, but her action caused her to collide with a solid male frame emerging like a tornado from within. The force of their collision knocked the loosely bound report file from her hands, scattering papers all over the place, and when she bent down hastily to retrieve them, she noticed that some of the papers obviously belonged to the man she had collided with.

'Clumsy girl!' a woman scolded Loren as the man went down on his haunches to retrieve his own papers as well as Loren's, and it had all happened so fast that Loren looked up then for the first time.

Mrs Markham, trim and well-dressed as always, stood glowering down at her, and Loren lowered her gaze with a sense of foreboding. She found herself looking into the incredibly blue, faintly annoyed eyes of Steve Beaumont, and her heart seemed to leap into her throat to choke off her breath. He was kneeling so close to her that her sensitive nose picked up the scent of his very masculine cologne and, for what seemed like interminable seconds, she felt too paralysed to do anything except stare into his deeply tanned, ruggedly handsome face.

'I'm—I'm most terribly sorry,' she stammered at length, flushed with embarrassment and annoyance.

'My fault entirely,' he said coldly but generously as he helped her restore order to the file of papers she had been carrying. 'You're new here, aren't you?'

'I've been here three weeks,' Loren informed him a little breathlessly. 'I'm Mr Griffin's secretary.'

'Ah, yes,' he murmured, not looking at her as he straightened his own batch of documents and rose to his full, imperious height. 'I think that's the lot.'

'Yes . . . thank you.'

She got unsteadily to her feet, and would have stepped beyond him into the lift, but his next remark sent a numbness shooting into her legs which made them stubbornly disobey the messages from her brain.

'I'm sure I've seen you somewhere before.' He was studying her contemplatively with a deep frown between his dark brows. 'Do I know your name?'

'It's Loren Fraser,' she heard herself saying, but she realised that this was not the time to enlighten him as to where he had seen her before.

'Loren,' he repeated her name thoughtfully in his deep-throated voice, and the sound of it sent an odd little shiver racing through her. 'Unusual name,' he added, his blue, thoughtful gaze sliding over her.

Mrs Markham murmured something to him which had him glancing swiftly at the expensive gold watch strapped to his strong wrist and, with no more than a brief inclination of his head in Loren's direction, he strode out of the building with Mrs Markham following him at her usual running pace.

CHAPTER TWO

LOREN was still shaky after her catastrophic encounter with Steve Beaumont when she reached the fourth floor and went in search of room 403. She had never been so clumsy in her life before, but neither had he looked where he was going when he had come barging out of the lift. They had both been at fault, but knowing this did not lessen her embarrassment.

The door to room 403 stood open, and a big, burly man with untidy grey hair rose from behind his desk when she knocked.

'Mr MacDonald?'

'Yes, come in,' he smiled in a cool, somewhat absent manner.

'I'm Loren Fraser, Mr Griffin's secretary,' she introduced herself when he gazed at her enquiringly. 'He asked me to bring these reports to you.'

'Thank you,' he nodded, taking the file from her and seating himself behind his desk once again. He flipped open the file to glance at the contents and, with no reason to linger, Loren turned towards the door. 'Just a minute!'

The sudden harshness in his voice made her swing round sharply. 'Is something wrong?'

He held up two single sheets of paper, and even at that distance she could see that the typed sheets could not possibly have come from the Accounts department.

'What are these papers doing in this file?' he demanded.

She went forward at once to study the papers more closely, but she had already guessed what had happened, and she went cold at the thought. 'I'm afraid I—I collided with Mr Beaumont outside the lift on the ground floor, and some of his documents must have got mixed up with the papers in that file.'

'*Damn!*' Jim MacDonald exploded so violently that Loren actually flinched and leapt back a pace.

'Are they important?' she asked anxiously, knowing the answer even before it was shouted at her.

'I'll say they're important. If he has any hopes of clinching that two million rand contract, then he can forget about it without these figures and information.'

'I shall have to take them to him at once,' she made a snap decision which Jim MacDonald did not contradict, and she almost snatched the vitally important documents out of his hand.

'Mr Beaumont is on his way to the airport, and if you hurry you might just make it before his plane leaves,' he said, reaching for the telephone on his desk. 'I'll let old Griffin know, and I'll have one of the company cars waiting for you at the entrance.'

'Thanks,' Loren flung the word at him as she darted towards the door and down the long, carpeted passage towards the lift.

She thumbed the button against the wall, cursing the lift for its slowness, and when the doors slid open, she almost fell into it in her haste to press the button for the ground floor. Nothing like this had ever happened to her before, she thought as she leaned against the carpeted wall close to the door. She had always prided herself on remaining calm in the most trying circumstances, yet here she was dashing about, literally and figuratively, like a frantic fly with a belly full of insecticide. Oh, why did everything always move at a snail's pace when one was in a hurry?

A dark blue Mercedes slid to a halt at the entrance to the building, and a Black driver leapt out of the driver's seat to open the rear door for her.

'Where to, madam?' he asked politely, and her glance went automatically to the name tag pinned to the jacket lapel of his uniform.

'How appropriate,' she laughed with a touch of nervous hysteria as she got into the car. 'To the airport, *James*, and don't spare the horse-power!'

He looked a bit taken aback by her manner, but he was aware of the urgency of this mission, and wasted no time in getting behind the wheel. The security gate officials had obviously been alerted, for the boom was raised as the Mercedes approached it, and they shot through it without the customary check.

Loren leaned back in her seat and tried to remain calm during the drive through the industrial area of the city, but her agitation was growing within her like a simmering volcano. She glanced continuously at her wrist watch. Five minutes had elapsed, then ten minutes since they had left the offices of Beaumont Engineering. She had no idea what flight he would be on, but she had a dreadful feeling that they were going to be too late if James did not hurry it up a little.

'Can't you go any faster?' she queried anxiously, leaning forward in her seat, and wishing she could sprout jet propelled wings.

'Madam, I'm going as fast as I can in this traffic,' James told her pointedly and, clutching those vitally important papers in her agitated hands, she fell back against the padded back rest and closed her eyes.

'Oh, lord, what a mess!' she groaned aloud, and her insides felt so knotted that she was certain they would never unravel themselves again.

Loren could barely contain herself when the airport building was in sight, and she was out of the car like a shot when James finally parked the Mercedes at the entrance to the departure lounge. She walked as fast as her high-heeled shoes would allow, almost running at

times as she pushed her way through people. She was
searching for the one man she had not been able to
forget entirely since she had first seen him, and then she
caught sight of him in a queue of passengers moving
swiftly through the security gates.

'Mr Beaumont!' she called, aware of heads turning
inquisitively in her direction, but not caring as she
darted towards him. 'Mr Beaumont, wait!'

Her heart was pounding against her ribs, and she felt
quite faint with relief when he turned his head and saw her.

'What is it this time?' he asked, raising a sardonic
eyebrow as he stepped out of the queue towards her,
and that hint of sarcasm in his voice did not escape her.

'These documents belong to you,' she explained,
almost thrusting them at him in her relief. 'Mr
MacDonald noticed them amongst the reports I'd taken
up to him, and I can only think I must have put them in
my file by mistake.'

'So he sent you careering across the city to bring
them here to me at the airport?'

'I volunteered, knowing the urgency of the matter,
and I was terribly afraid I might miss you,' Loren told
him, withstanding the scrutiny of his cool blue eyes.

'I'd better make sure I haven't any of your papers
tucked away amongst mine,' he said, opening his
briefcase and placing the documents she had given him
into it before he looked through the rest of his papers.
'Yes, here's something.'

He held out three neatly typed sheets of figures which
belonged to the Chief Accountant's report, and when she
took them he snapped his briefcase shut decisely.

'I really am most dreadfully sorry,' she apologised,
feeling quite ill at ease suddenly, and somewhat foolish.

'Are you sorry?'

His mocking smile was disconcerting, and she looked
away, directly into the eyes of an official who appeared

to be attempting to catch Steve Beaumont's attention. 'I think they're waiting for you to go through, Mr Beaumont.'

He gestured to the official that he was on his way, then he nodded briefly in her direction. 'Thank you, Miss Fraser.'

She stood there watching him disappear through the security entrance, and only then did she turn away. Her legs felt like jelly and her insides were shaking as she walked towards the exit of the departure lounge, but she put it down to the anxiety of the past half hour, and tried not to think of how very nearly she had been the cause of a disaster which would have lost the company a two million rand contract.

Instead of being annoyed, as he would have had every right to be, Harvey Griffin appeared to find the incident highly amusing, and she had to relate every detail to him from the moment she had left the office with his report. He laughed so much in the end that he had to remove his spectacles to wipe the tears from his eyes, and Loren, who had found nothing amusing about the anxiety she had suffered, eyed him warily until he had managed to control himself.

'It wouldn't have been a laughing matter if Mr Beaumont had gone off without those documents, and I ought to warn you to be more careful in future, but——' He glanced at Loren a little sheepishly as he replaced his spectacles, 'all's well that ends well, and we'll leave it at that.'

His grin was infectious and, without intending to, she found herself grinning back at him, then she excused herself and made a second trip up to the fourth floor with the papers Steve Beaumont had given her at the airport, and this time she completed the errand without a hitch.

'What happened to you this afternoon?' Natalie

wanted to know when Loren gave her a lift home that afternoon. 'I called in to see you, and all I could get out of Mr Griffin was that you'd gone to the airport.'

'It was a near-disaster,' Loren told her, her insides still tightening at the memory as she related the incident to Natalie.

'I'll bet Mrs Markham has pups when she finds out,' Natalie laughed. 'She's terribly fussy where Mr Beaumont is concerned, and everything has to be *just so*, if not *better*.'

'Well, as you know, she already thinks I'm a clumsy idiot.'

'It could happen to anyone.'

'But why to me?' Loren groaned, her hands tightening on the steering wheel in sheer nervous reaction.

When they arrived at Natalie's flat, Loren was invited in to have coffee with Natalie and her mother, and Mrs Miller was such a homely woman that Loren was instantly relaxed in her company.

'Why don't you stay and have dinner with us?' Mrs Miller suggested when Loren wanted to leave. 'I know what you young girls are like. You don't cook a decent meal for yourselves, and end up eating all the wrong food.'

'I accept your invitation, Mrs Miller,' Loren laughed as she resumed her seat. 'I was going home to a salad this evening, but whatever it is you're cooking, it smells tremendously appetising.'

'It's a cold evening, so I've made a pot of soup, and a mutton stew,' the older woman smiled.

'Mutton stew!' Loren echoed with a sigh, licking her lips mentally in anticipation. 'That sounds like home.'

'Mutton is very expensive in Johannesburg these days,' Mrs Miller remarked conversationally when Natalie and Loren followed her into the kitchen to help her.

'If the drought continues in the Karoo it's bound to become scarce as well,' Loren added, seeing in her mind the dry, dusty Karoo veld she loved so much.

She told them about her parents and about the problems the sheep farmers were encountering during this severe drought, but no one could remain serious for long in Natalie's buoyant company. They talked and laughed a lot throughout dinner, and also while the dishes were being washed and packed away. They had coffee afterwards in the lounge with its old but comfortable furniture, and Loren realised that the tensions of the day had drained from her almost completely.

The ringing of the telephone finally intruded on their conversation and Natalie got up to answer it. Loren glanced at her wrist watch. Seven-thirty? She had been there two hours, and she did not want to abuse their hospitality.

'That was my boy-friend, Peter,' said Natalie when she put down the receiver. 'He's coming round for a while.'

'Well, I must be on my way,' said Loren, getting to her feet to collect her coat and her handbag.

'You don't have to leave in such a hurry, you know,' Natalie laughed at Loren.

'I know,' Loren smiled at her. 'I've had a wonderful time, for which I must thank you and your mother, but I still have a few things to do before I can think of going to bed this evening.'

'You're welcome to come and have dinner with us again at any time,' the older woman offered generously.

'You're very kind, Mrs Miller, and I thank you.'

Natalie accompanied Loren down to where she had parked her Stanza, and when Loren slid into the driver's seat, Natalie leaned forward to say, 'Thanks for the lift, and see you tomorrow.'

'I hope I still have a job tomorrow,' Loren laughed wryly as she turned the key in the ignition, then she waved and drove herself through the brightly lit streets of the city to her own flat.

There was no sense in brooding over what had happened that day, but a week later she was forced to recall her mad dash across the city to the airport, and this time in more humiliating circumstances.

Harvey Griffin buzzed her from his office, and his voice crackled over the line when she lifted the receiver of the intercom system on her desk. 'Miss Fraser, would you order two cups of coffee from the canteen and bring it through to my office when it arrives?'

'Yes, Mr Griffin, I'll do so at once,' Loren replied politely.

She ordered the coffee, and ten minutes later a Black woman entered her office after knocking tentatively on the door.

'The coffee, madam,' she said, placing the tray on Loren's desk.

'Thank you,' Loren smiled up at her quickly.

'Do you want me to pour?'

If Loren had had any premonition of what was to follow, she would have sent this neatly clad woman from the canteen into Harvey Griffin's office with the coffee, but instead she shook her head and said: 'I'll pour when I've taken it through to Mr Griffin, thank you.'

The woman left, and Loren pushed back her typewriter to take the tray through to the office adjoining hers. She knocked on the interlinking door and opened it without waiting for a reply, but she almost dropped the tray when she saw Steve Beaumont seated in the chair on the opposite side of Harvey Griffin's desk. She would recognise that dark, mahogany head and wide shoulders anywhere, and when he turned to settle his piercing blue gaze on her she was totally disconcerted by it.

'Ah, Miss Fraser,' Harvey Griffin remarked with the very slightest hint of amusement in his voice as she placed the tray on the corner of his desk. 'I believe you've met Mr Beaumont.'

'We have met, yes,' Loren replied, annoyed with herself for blushing like a schoolgirl, and unable to meet that assessing blue gaze which she felt certain was filled with mockery. 'How do you take your coffee, Mr Beaumont?'

'Black with no sugar.'

His deep-throated voice had the oddest effect on her nerve-ends. It made them quiver in response like violin strings which had been plucked, and it made her feel quite strange.

She added sugar and milk to Harvey Griffin's coffee as she knew he liked it, then she turned towards Steve Beaumont with his cup of black coffee. His unfaltering gaze disturbed her to the point of nervousness, and at that moment the toe of her high-heeled shoe kicked against the protruding roll in the carpet. She lost her balance and succeeded in steadying herself almost at once, but that was more than she could say for the cup of steaming black coffee she held in her outstretched hand. The cup seemed to catapult from the saucer, and Steve Beaumont caught it smartly, but not before the contents had spilled on to his left thigh. Loren stood mortified as he leapt to his feet with a curse on his lips, and his eyes on the swiftly spreading stain on the pants of his immaculate light-grey suit.

'Oh, I'm most dreadfully sorry, Mr Beaumont,' she managed when at last she found her voice. 'I'll get a cloth, and I'll——'

'Leave it!' he snapped, his expression grim with pain and annoyance as he turned towards Harvey Griffin who had risen concernedly behind his desk. 'This carpet of yours should have been seen to long ago, Harvey. I suggest you put in a requisition at once.'

'Yes, Mr Beaumont, sir.'

'I'll get you another cup of coffee, Mr Beaumont,' Loren offered, her hands shaking so much with the after-effects of shock that she could barely hold the cup steady which he had passed to her.

'Forget it!' he barked, his eyes narrowed and cold as they slid over her, then he glanced at Harvey Griffin. 'We'll discuss that matter some other time.'

He strode out of the office, using the passage entrance, and Loren felt as if her legs wanted to give way beneath her when he closed the door firmly behind his tall frame.

'Oh dear!' she breathed miserably. 'I guess I've really done it this time, haven't I?'

'You certainly have, Miss Fraser.' Harvey Griffin lowered himself into his chair with a long-suffering sigh. 'First you nearly lose him a two million rand contract, and now ... well, I don't think anyone would appreciate having themselves scalded with hot coffee.'

'What can I say?' Loren gestured helplessly.

'It was an accident,' her boss assured her, 'and as Mr Beaumont pointed out, this carpet should have been seen to long ago.'

Loren had never felt so terrible about anything in her life before. This was the second disaster which had occurred to her since working for Beaumont Engineering, and on both occasions it had involved the big chief himself. Calm and efficient, Matt Kruger had always called her, but she was neither of those things at the moment.

'I'll clear up this mess,' she sighed, carrying out the tray and going in search of a cloth to wipe the chair and the desk where the coffee had splashed.

'You're looking a bit peaky this afternoon,' Natalie remarked, noticing Loren's unusual pallor when she came in to see her some time later.

'You're not going to believe this,' Loren warned her. 'I spilled the entire contents of a cup of scalding coffee in Mr Beaumont's lap this afternoon.'

Natalie raised her hands to her mouth, and her eyes widened in dismay. 'Oh, lord, no!'

'Oh, lord, yes!' Loren mimicked her with a wry smile. 'My foot hooked on a roll in the carpet, I lost my balance for a moment, and the cup simply went flying out of the saucer.'

Natalie surfaced from her initial shock and giggled. 'I wish I could have seen it.'

'I wish I was dead!' Loren groaned, burying her face in her hands for a moment. 'Besides his being scalded, I'm sure I've ruined his suit.'

'Cheer up,' Natalie told her, perching herself on the corner of the desk. 'Steve Beaumont has oodles of money with which to replace the one you might have ruined.'

'That doesn't make me feel any better.'

'What did old Griffin do?'

Loren snorted disparagingly. 'He simply stood there imitating a statue, but I could swear he was laughing inside.'

'That man has an odd sense of humour, I admit, but why don't you follow his example and laugh about it?' Natalie asked with a wicked twinkle in her dark eyes.

'If I laugh now I'll end up crying,' Loren confessed miserably. 'Honesty, Natalie, I've never known myself to be so clumsy.'

She stared at her typewriter, but all she could see was that dark stain spreading across the leg of Steve Beaumont's pants, and she felt herself shrivel up inside with mortification.

'To change the subject,' Natalie said brightly, 'do you think you could give me a lift home this afternoon? I've had to take my car to the garage for a check-up.'

'Again?' Loren frowned up at her.

'Again,' Natalie laughed. 'And my mother said I was to tell you she has cottage pie for dinner this evening.'

Loren smiled for the first time since Natalie had walked into her office. 'That sounds much too tempting an invitation to resist.'

'See you later, then.'

Loren somehow managed to settle down to her work, but it was only at Natalie's home that evening that she relaxed and shook off the after-effects of spilling coffee all over the chief of Beaumont Engineering. He had been annoyed, and rightly so, and she could well imagine what he must be thinking of her. *Incompetent* and *clumsy* were two adjectives that came to mind, and no amount of self-recrimination could undo the wrong that had been done on two consecutive occasions.

Loren had to work late one evening the following week on an urgent report which Jim MacDonald had requested from Harvey Griffin, and it was after six o'clock that evening when she pulled the last sheet of paper from her typewriter. She arranged the typed sheets in their proper order and slipped them into a file and, taking her handbag and her coat with her, she left her office and took the lift up to the fourth floor to leave the file on Jim MacDonald's desk where he would find it first thing in the morning.

The building was almost ominously quiet at that time of the evening with everyone gone, but when Loren walked out of Jim MacDonald's office she discovered that she was not the only one who had worked late, and her nerves reacted sharply at the sight of Steve Beaumont approaching the lift from the opposite direction. She had dreaded having to face him again, but now there was no way of avoiding it, she realised as she reached the lift before him and pressed the button.

'After you, Miss Fraser,' he said when the lift doors slid open and he saw her hesitate. The panther-like tread of his powerful frame had stirred an animal instinct within her, and she was tempted to take flight down the stairs, but that would have been ridiculous, and she swallowed nervously as she stepped into the lift cage ahead of him. The doors slid shut, closeting them together in that confined space, and when he pressed the ground floor button she sought desperately for something to say to break the awkward silence between them, but it was Steve Beaumont who spoke first. 'You're working late this evening?'

'I had an urgent report to type which Mr Griffin and Mr MacDonald wanted on his desk first thing in the morning,' she explained, clutching her handbag and her coat against her as if it were a shield against the onslaught of raw masculinity which seemed to emanate from this man.

'I see,' he nodded.

She felt his eyes on her, cool and appraising, but she stared straight ahead of her as she gathered the necessary courage to say what had to be said. 'Mr Beaumont, I—I really am sorry about the other day. Your suit must be ruined, and I do hope I didn't scald you too badly.'

Out of the corner of her eye she saw him raise a sardonic eyebrow. 'My suit has been returned as good as new from the cleaners, and as you see, I've survived the ordeal.'

'I don't know what——' She broke off abruptly, gripping the rail beside her as the lift cage shuddered and came to a grinding halt between two floors, and she darted a nervous glance at her companion. 'What has happened? What's wrong?'

'An electrical fault,' he said, thumbing several buttons on the steel panel.

'Isn't there something you can do?'

'I've done everything possible except ring the emergency bell, and that's precisely what I'm going to do now,' he explained with a calmness that made her want to scream, and moments later she could hear a bell ringing shrilly somewhere in the building.

'Do you think someone might hear it?' she asked into the ensuing silence while she shrank into the farthest corner away from Steve Beaumont.

'Someone might.'

'And if they don't?'

'If there's no one but us left in the building, then we shall simply have to wait until the night watchman makes his rounds at nine-thirty before we ring this bell again to attract his attention.'

'But we can't stay here closeted in this thing for simply hours!' she argued frantically.

'Do you have any bright suggestions on how to get out of here?'

His sarcasm stung, and she fell back into the corner of the lift with a groan. 'Oh, lord!'

'The moment we got into this lift together I should have known something like this might happen,' he accused mockingly, putting down his briefcase and folding his arms across his wide chest as he surveyed her with narrowed eyes. 'I'm beginning to think you're a walking disaster, Miss Fraser.'

Loren coloured with embarrassment. 'I don't suppose I can blame you for thinking that.'

'Do you suppose there's a possibility that we might meet in future without something disastrous happening?'

'At the moment I very much doubt it,' she laughed out of sheer nervousness, and felt herself caught in the grip of an odd tension at the thought of having to spend the next few hours alone with this man who was observing her so intently. 'Don't you think you ought to ring that emergency bell again?'

His eyebrows rose mockingly above those incredibly blue eyes. 'I assure you it rings very loudly throughout the building. If there's still someone about to hear it, then we shall be out of here within the next hour, but if there's no one——'

'We'll have to wait for the night watchman's round at nine-thirty,' she finished for him with a sigh of resignation passing her lips.

'Exactly!' His eyes mocked her, but she was almost certain that she glimpsed a hint of annoyance in the smile that curved his strongly sensuous mouth. 'Is there someone expecting you home early? Someone who might be concerned if you don't arrive on time?'

'There's no one.'

'Then you have nothing to worry about,' he said in a clipped voice, but he was wrong. She had plenty to worry about while they stood there in opposite corners staring at the door which had locked them so firmly together in that confined space.

She wished now that she had reacted on her initial instinct to take the stairs instead of the lift, but it was a futile wish. Steve Beaumont had called her a walking disaster, and she was becoming convinced that, where he was concerned, that was exactly what she had become.

'I feel almost as if I ought to apologise to you for this inconvenience,' she smiled up at him wryly.

'I doubt if it will help,' he laughed shortly, and it was a pleasant sound that brushed across her frayed nerves, then he glanced at his wrist watch and sighed. 'It looks as if we're going to have a long wait, so we might as well make ourselves comfortable.'

He lowered himself on to the carpeted floor, and Loren reluctantly followed his example, edging herself into the corner for a comfortable back rest. It was going to be a long wait, as he had said, and heaven only knew how they were going to pass the time.

She studied him unobtrusively, taking in the muscular thighs straining against the expensive woollen fabric of his dark pants, and she lowered her glance slowly to the genuine leather of his shoes. He raised his right hand, and her eyes followed the movement as if hypnotised to see him loosen his tie and undo the top button of his white silk shirt. She had been wrong about the colour of his hair. In the light above them it shone like burnished copper, and she wondered what it would feel like to run her fingers through it.

Loren reined in her thoughts sharply, alarmed at herself, and she directed her gaze away from him to stare at the doors, willing them to open, or *something*. She had to get out of here ... but how?

'There's not a female in this company who wouldn't give her false eyelashes for just five minutes alone with him,' Natalie's remark filtered through Loren's mind, and she almost laughed out loud. If most women were dying to spend just five minutes with him, then *she* certainly was not one of them, but here she was trapped with him in a lift for presumably several hours, and all she wanted to do was to get away from him.

'I believe you come from a place called Aberdeen which is somewhere in a godforsaken part of the Karoo,' Steve Beaumont interrupted her thoughts.

'The Karoo is not godforsaken!' she exclaimed indignantly, forgetting for the moment who he was. 'At the moment there's a severe drought, but after a good rainy season it's one of the most beautiful places on this earth.'

His blue eyes mocked her. 'If you nurse such intense feelings for that semi-desert part of the country, then why did you leave it?'

'I needed a change.'

'Did the monotony of life there get you down, or was it a man?'

He was coming so close to the truth that she had to force herself to remain cool and calm as she met his derisive glance levelly. 'Are you trying to make me angry, Mr Beaumont?'

'I'm trying to find some way of passing the time,' he smiled twistedly, and the look in his eyes did something to her insides that made her lower her gaze hastily.

'Careful, Loren,' she warned herself. 'You're beginning to imagine things, and that could be dangerous in the circumstances.'

Her advice to herself was sound, but she had to admit that she had never been so acutely conscious of any man before in her life. An aura of masculinity surrounded him, making her aware of a powerful but leashed sensuality. She looked up to find his gaze moving with a slow, sensual deliberation from her glossy hair which was coiled into a knot in the nape of her neck, down to her pearl grey shoes, and she had the most alarming feeling that his eyes were invading her body beneath the neat grey suit and crisp white blouse. It made the breath catch in her throat, and the blood surged into her face to heighten the sparkle of annoyance in her eyes. He had no right to look at her like that, it was positively indecent, but her anger diminished rapidly when she made the frightening discovery that a part of her actually welcomed his somewhat intimate scrutiny. It made her aware of her own femininity as nothing and no one had ever done before, but it also made her aware of an element of danger which was developing between her and this man with whom she was sharing this forced imprisonment.

CHAPTER THREE

'TELL me about yourself,' Steve Beaumont intruded on Loren's turbulent thoughts, and she almost jumped nervously at the sound of his deep-throated voice.

'I was born on a farm near Aberdeen in the Karoo, and I've lived there all my life except for the two years I was away at secretarial college,' she skimmed briefly and reluctantly over her past.

'Is that all?' he mocked her when she fell silent, and she had difficulty in avoiding his disturbing eyes.

'If you know I come from Aberdeen, then you must also know I've been working for an attorney for the past four years, and what else is there to tell you?'

'Boy-friends?' he asked bluntly, his smile deepening.

'There've been several,' she lied airily.

'I'm surprised none of them have snapped you up and married you, but instead your file tells me you're twenty-five and still free.'

'I'm not ready for marriage.' She slanted a glance at him, surprised that he should have gone to the trouble of examining her personal file. 'Are you married, Mr Beaumont?' she asked before she could stop herself.

'No,' he replied somewhat abruptly, pulling up one leg and resting his arm on his knee as he turned slightly to face her. 'In my kind of a job a wife would be nothing more than a nuisance. I travel a lot, I have to, and a wife's tears and tantrums would merely interfere with my work, or bore me to distraction.'

His attitude disturbed her, and she wondered why, but she could not find an explanation for it. 'If you found the right woman I'm sure she would understand,

and there'd be no need for tears or tantrums whenever you go away on business.'

'I have no intention of looking for the right woman,' he stated bluntly. 'I like my freedom. It allows me to come and go as I please, and when I tire of one woman I turf her out of my life and find myself another. It's as simple as that.'

'I see,' she murmured, quite appalled by the glimpse he had given her into his personal and very private life.

'I sense your disapproval.'

'I'm not in a position to approve or disapprove, Mr Beaumont,' she assured him, her eyes cool when they met his. 'What you do with your life is entirely your own business.'

'My sentiments exactly,' he smiled derisively, and they lapsed into a chilly little silence which Loren shattered some minutes later when she pushed back the sleeve of her jacket.

'Damn!' she muttered softly. 'My watch has stopped.'

'It's a quarter to seven,' Steve Beaumont informed her with a suggestion of a frown between his dark brows. 'I'm afraid we still have a long wait ahead of us.'

'It feels as if we've already been here for hours,' she sighed, altering her position slightly to make herself more comfortable.

'I can't shake the feeling that we've met somewhere before,' he remarked, raising a quizzical eyebrow at her. 'Have we?'

Loren vividly recalled her first evening in Johannesburg, and smiled faintly. 'I wouldn't exactly say that we've met before, but you were having dinner in the restaurant of the Metropolitan Hotel one evening about five weeks ago, and——'

'And you were dining alone at a table close to mine,' he concluded her explanation for her, his brow clearing. 'I remember now. Your hair wasn't tied up the way it is now, and you were wearing a yellowish-brown dress that matched the gold flecks in your eyes.'

Her heart missed an uncomfortable beat. 'You couldn't possibly have noticed the colour of my eyes at that distance.'

'I can see their colour now, can't I?' he argued, leaning towards her and looking directly into her eyes for a brief moment before she veiled them with her lashes. 'Are you still staying at the Metropolitan?'

'No,' she shook her head and tried desperately to control that inward tremor which had been aroused by his disturbing nearness. 'I've moved into a flat belonging to Natalie Miller's sister and brother-in-law. They're away for three months, and I'm renting it from them.'

'I see.' He was silent for a moment, then he grimaced. 'Talking about the Metropolitan has made me realise that I haven't had anything to eat all day, and a succulent piece of steak would go down well at this moment.'

Loren had skipped lunch that day, and the mention of food made her aware that she had a hollow feeling at the pit of her stomach.

'I have half a bar of chocolate in my handbag, if you'd like to share it with me,' she offered hesitantly, and he slanted that attractive smile at her that made her feel as if she was melting inside.

'That's very kind of you, Miss Fraser.'

Loren shared the chocolate between them, and neither of them spoke until the last piece had melted away in their mouths. Her mind cruelly conjured up a cool, thirst-quenching glass of water, and when she grimaced she found Steve Beaumont's questioning glance resting on her.

'I should have remembered that eating chocolate always makes me thirsty,' she explained with a selfconscious laugh.

'This time I am in a position to help you,' he said, opening his briefcase and producing a slim silver flask.

'What is it?' she asked when he he had removed the top and was holding the flask out to her.

'Brandy,' he said, shifting his position, and his arm brushed against hers unexpectedly, setting every nerve in her body tingling in the wake of that brief contact. 'It will settle your nerves.'

'I'm not nervous,' she argued, taking the flask from him.

'If you're not nervous, then why are your hands shaking?'

She cursed him silently for noticing the devastating effect his nearness was having on her, and she tried to explain it away. 'I'm tired, that's all.'

'Then I suggest you take a mouthful of this,' he insisted, placing his hand over hers and raising the flask to her lips.

She obligingly took a mouthful, but it slid down her throat like liquid fire, taking her breath away momentarily and making her cough and splutter. 'It's absolutely vile!'

'It will make you feel better in a minute, though,' he laughed shortly, forcing her to swallow down a second mouthful, but this time she was prepared for the taste and sting of the brandy, and it went down a little easier.

'I don't feel better, I feel dizzy,' she complained seconds later when it felt as if the lift were tilting about her.

'Put your head back and relax,' he advised, draining the flask and screwing on the top before he returned it to his briefcase.

'Are you sure that was pure brandy you gave me, and nothing more?' she asked with a hint of humour in her voice as she settled her head comfortably in the corner and closed her eyes.

'I don't drug my women before I seduce them, and when I practise seduction I prefer the comfort of a bed every time.'

Of all the replies he could have given, that was the most unexpected, and when she raised her strangely heavy eyelids in shocked surprise, she found herself looking straight into a pair of mocking blue eyes barely inches from her own. He had introduced a certain intimacy into the atmosphere, and she felt her blood quicken its pace through her veins.

'Have you seduced many women?' she asked without thinking, and his soft, throaty laughter sent a wave of hot colour surging into her cheeks.

'You're obviously not quite sober, or you wouldn't have asked that question,' he observed shrewdly.

'You're quite right,' she confessed, wrenching her eyes from his. 'I'm not used to anything stronger than wine, and then I seldom have more than half a glass.'

'Have you ever been seduced, Loren Fraser?'

Her senses responded to that low, vibrant note of seduction in his voice, but her mind was still clear enough to reject it. 'Not that I can recall.'

'What kind of an answer is that?' he demanded.

'It means that I don't indulge in bedroom capers.'

Strong fingers beneath her chin forced her to meet his compelling eyes. 'You've never slept with a man before?'

'No,' she answered truthfully, her cheeks burning, then she laughed softly at the expression that flitted across his ruggedly handsome features. 'Don't look so surprised, Mr Beaumont. Down Aberdeen way that sort of thing simply isn't done unless one is married.'

'Is that why you left Aberdeen?' he questioned her with a derisive twist to his mouth. 'Because you would like to go to bed with a man without anyone having something to say about it?'

'Most certainly not!' she exclaimed indignantly, brushing his hand away when the deliberate caress of his fingers against her cheek sent a quivering warmth cascading through her body.

'I was merely asking,' he shrugged, moving a little away from her to study her with frowning intensity. 'Why *did* you leave the safety of Aberdeen to come to this big bad city?'

He was laughing at her, she was aware of that, but she was determined not to let her annoyance show. 'There were problems.'

'What sort of problems?' he pounced on her reply, and she smiled cynically.

'I'm twenty-five, as you so rightly pointed out earlier, and everyone thought it was time I found myself a husband. They made it so embarrassingly obvious what they were hoping for every time I went out with a man that in the end I refused every invitation that came my way, except when that invitation came from Matt Kruger.'

'Matt Kruger?'

'He's the attorney I worked for,' she explained, wondering how he had missed that bit of information on her personal file. 'Matt understood what I was going through, and he was very supportive, but eventually it became an embarrassment even to be seen with him.' She paused and frowned at the man seated beside her. 'I don't know why I'm telling you this, because it's really none of your business, you know.'

'It's the brandy,' he grinned.

'It must be,' she agreed, feeling suddenly so totally relaxed that she could not believe she was in the company of a virtual stranger. 'How did Beaumont Engineering come about?' she questioned him in turn.

'My father started the company, and I took over the reins six years ago after his death.'

'And your mother?'

'She died when I was in my teens, and my father never married again.' A gleam of mockery entered his eyes as he turned his head to glance at her. 'He lived with a woman for quite a number of years, and after his death she went to Namibia to live with her widowed sister.'

He had intended to shock her, but she had somehow progressed beyond that. 'Why didn't your father marry her?'

'There was no reason for him to do that,' Steve Beaumont smiled twistedly. 'They had a perfect relationship going between them. My father gave her all the security she needed while he was still alive, and after his death she received a large sum of money which ought to keep her in style for the remainder of her life.'

'What if there'd been a child?'

'I guess he would have made it legitimate,' Steve Beaumont shrugged off her irrelevant query. 'Who can tell?'

They fell silent, and his brooding expression made her wonder whether she had not perhaps pried too deeply into his personal life, but then she could not recall that he had asked permission to pry into hers.

'What's the time?' she asked eventually, and he flicked back the cuff of his jacket.

'Almost eight o'clock.'

'Another hour and a half,' she sighed tiredly.

'Does my company bore you?' he mocked her.

'Not at all,' she answered truthfully, but she winced inwardly at the pins and needles in her bottom. 'The floor is getting rather hard, and I've always hated the thought of being cooped up in tiny rooms.'

'Was your father always a sheep farmer?' Steve Beaumont queried, and she could not decide whether he was merely making an attempt to help the time pass, or whether he was actually interested.

'Yes, always,' she replied abruptly. 'Like his father before him, and so on.'

'I gather the farm has been in the family for generations, then?'

'It has,' she confirmed. 'My father has added to it in his lifetime, and it now covers a much larger area than the original farm.'

'And your mother?' he questioned her now as she had questioned him earlier.

'My mother came from the city,' she explained. 'My father injured his back when a horse threw him, and he was sent to Port Elizabeth where they put him in traction for some weeks. My mother was a nursing Sister at the hospital, and that's how they met.'

A faintly derisive smile curved his mouth. 'How did a city girl adapt to farm life, I wonder?'

'She adapted very well, and professionally she's always in demand among the people in the farming community.' Loren paused momentarily for thought, then added: 'My mother has never given the impression that she craves a different sort of life from that on the farm, and my parents are absolutely devoted to each other.'

'How are you adapting to city life?' he asked with a strangely wicked gleam in his eyes.

'Very well, so far,' she confessed truthfully. 'I miss the wide open spaces, and that feeling of being among old and familiar friends when I walk down the street, but other than that I'm quite content.'

'Do you miss your Matt Kruger?'

'He's not *my* Matt Kruger, but ... yes, I miss him.' She was annoyed with herself when she felt her cheeks grow warm beneath his scrutiny. 'You don't work alongside someone for four years and then simply forget them in a flash.'

He nodded slowly as if he understood and agreed,

then he glanced at her speculatively. 'I don't want to make this situation more unbearable for you than it already is, but would you object if I lit a cigarette?'

'Please go ahead,' she said at once, surprised that he had abstained from smoking out of consideration for her.

He selected a cigarette from a slim gold cigarette case, and in the flame of his lighter his features took on ruthless proportions. He drew hard on his cigarette and inhaled deeply, the he exhaled the smoke through his nostrils in thin twin jets. He had nice hands, she thought, observing him unobrusively. The nails were clean and clipped short, and fine dark hairs were like a shadow on the back of his hands. They were strong, male hands; hands that could control and crush, and caress a woman with equal skill and experience.

There I go again, thinking the most absurd thoughts! she chided herself angrily, but there was something about Steve Beaumont that made her thoughts run freely along an avenue she had never felt the desire to explore before, and every instinct within her warned of the danger in this digression from the normal. He was an attractive man, she could not deny this to herself, but then so was Matt Kruger, and several other men she had known in the past. What, she wondered curiously, made Steve Beaumont so different?

He pushed the butt of his cigarette into the sand box close to him, and stretched his long legs comfortably. He appeared to be relaxed, but he was such a vital-looking man that she had the distinct impression his muscles were tensed and ready the instant action might be required.

Loren closed her eyes and tried to relax, but her own body was tense, and her nerves felt as taut as the strips of leather stretched across the seats of her mother's dining-room chairs. Despite her tension, however, she actually felt herself drifting into an uneasy sleep from which she was eventually roused by the muffled sound of heavy footsteps. She listened intently, but when she did not hear it again she decided that it must have been her imagination, and she did not stir from her relaxed position.

'Are you asleep?' Steve Beaumont's deep voice invaded her still drowsy state, but she was reluctant to emerge from it.

'No,' she murmured without opening her eyes.

'I think I hear the night watchman prowling around.'

That roused her instantly to complete alertness. 'Is it nine-thirty?'

He glanced at his wrist watch. 'It's a few minutes after nine, and he doesn't always make his rounds at exactly the same time.'

'How long do you think it will take to get us out of here?' she asked as he got to his feet and pressed the alarm.

'I believe the lift technicians are usually very quick to respond to a call, so I doubt if it will take longer than forty-five minutes at the most.' He held out his hands and smiled down at her mockingly as he drew her to her feet. 'Your ordeal of being closeted in here with me is almost over.'

'Almost,' she echoed when he released her hands, but she had a strange feeling that she was on the threshold of a far greater ordeal, and it was an ordeal which she would not find quite so easy to cope with.

They did not sit down again, but remained standing to ease off the stiffness in their limbs, and it seemed as if another eternity had passed before they hard the sound of a commotion on the floor above them. There were raised voices and a clattering of tools, and some minutes later a male voice could be heard quite distinctly through the air vents above them.

'Hello! Are you all right in there?'

'Yes,' Steve Beaumont barked. 'Just get us out of this damn thing, will you?'

'You'll be out in a jiffy, sir,' the technician above them reacted to the authoritative note in the voice of the man standing beside Loren.

'It won't be long now,' Steve Beaumont assured Loren with a strangely distant smile which seemed to sever the closeness they had shared during the past hours, and it made her feel extraordinarily lonely as she picked up her coat and her handbag to await their release from this prison to which they had been confined so unexpectedly.

The tinkering sounds above them ceased some minutes later, and Loren held her breath during the brief silence that elapsed before she felt the lift cage come to life beneath her and descend with painful slowness to the ground floor. The doors slid open reluctantly, like a predatory animal being forced to relinquish its prey, and relief washed over her when she could step out of the lift with Steve Beaumont's hand protectively beneath her elbow. The technician was apologetic, his eyes darting speculatively in Loren's direction, but Steve thanked him abruptly and ushered her out of the building to where she had parked her Stanza.

'I'll follow you in my car to make sure you get home safely,' he said as she unlocked the door and slid behind the wheel.

'That's very kind of you, but——'

'Don't argue,' he interrupted in a clipped voice, and, closing her door for her, he strode across the well-lit parking garages towards a tomato red Jaguar.

Loren sighed inwardly and turned the key in the ignition with shaky fingers. A few minutes later she was desperately trying to convince the suspicious security guard at the gate that her late departure had nothing to do with petty pilfering from the company.

The red Jaguar stopped behind her, its headlights illuminating the interior of her car just as the security guard was demanding her keys to search the Stanza's boot, and she heard Steve Beaumont's authoritative voice say clearly and abruptly, 'It's all right, Baker. We're here together.'

'Yes, sir,' the man replied at once, stepping back from her car and saluting respectfully, but the look he gave Loren made her feel as if she had emerged from an intimate and illicit *tête-à-tête* with Steve Beaumont. 'I'll lift the boom for you, lady.'

The boom was raised, and a few moments later she was driving through the industrial area towards the centre of the city with the red Jaguar's headlights almost blinding her in the rear-view mirror.

Steve Beaumont was not satisfied with merely making sure that she arrived safely at the building which housed her flat. He followed her down into the basement where she parked her car and, despite her protestations, he accompanied her up to the ninth floor. Outside her door, however, he bade her an abrupt 'goodnight', and she did not wait to see him go down in the lift.

Loren felt as if she had lived through a nightmare, but she did not want to dwell on it. It was after ten o'clock, and all she wanted to do was to go to bed and forget about the past four hours. She bathed quickly and put on her nightdress, but the doorbell rang before she could switch off the lights. Thinking it might be Natalie, Loren hastily put on her gown and tied the belt firmly about her waist, but she left the safety chain intact when she opened the door.

'I'm from Toni's Restaurant and Take-Aways,' said the young man on her doorstep, and he held out a bulky packet for her inspection. 'I was asked to deliver this to a Miss Fraser.'

Loren stared at him, bewildered and confused. 'But I didn't place an order at your restaurant for anything to be delivered here.'

'A gentleman placed the order, miss, and he asked me to give you this note,' the young man explained, passing her a folded sheet of paper through the small opening of the door.

Loren stared at the note in her hand, and only then did she realise that she could not leave the young man standing there holding the package. 'Just a minute.'

She undid the safety chain and opened the door wider to accept the package from him, and he smiled and said: '*Bon appétit*, miss.'

He was gone before she could thank him or tip him, and she locked the door securely before she went into the kitchen. She placed the package on the table and stared at the note she still clutched in her hand. This was from Steve Beaumont, she knew it, and when she unfolded the note her suspicions were confirmed. The bold, masculine handwriting seemed to leap out at her from the paper as she read the brief note warily.

I took the liberty of deciding you are as hungry as I am. Please accept this with my compliments. S.B.

A smile plucked at the corners of Loren's mouth as she slipped the note into the pocket of her robe, and removed the polystyrene container from the package. She lifted the lid to find it lined inside with plastic, and she sniffed at the delicious aroma of its contents. There was a portion of steak with mushroom sauce, baked potatoes, and a salad. It was still piping hot, and quite suddenly she was ravenous. She took out a knife and a fork, and sat down at the kitchen table to enjoy this unexpected meal, silently blessing Steve Beaumont for thinking of her. When she eventually went to bed that night she slept as if she had taken a sedative.

At the luncheon table in the canteen the following day, Loren pushed aside her plate and poured their tea. When she passed Natalie a cup she saw, not for the first time, an almost speculative look in her friend's eyes.

'Why are you looking at me so strangely?' she questioned Natalie, and the younger girl lowered her gaze guiltily.

'I'm trying to make up my mind whether I should tell you or not.'

'Tell me what, for goodness' sake?' Loren laughed with a mixture of exasperation and humour.

'I've heard a rumour that you were trapped for several hours in the lift last night with the big chief,' Natalie explained her odd behaviour.

'That's true,' Loren confirmed gravely. 'I worked late on that report for Mr MacDonald, and I took it up to his office as he'd requested. Mr Beaumont left his office at that time, and . . . well, you obviously know the rest.'

Natalie shifted uncomfortably in her chair. 'I must warn you, Loren, that there's a considerable amount of unkind speculation wafting about from one office to the next.'

'I suppose I should have expected something like this,' Loren sighed angrily, wondering why she had thought it would be different in a city such as Johannesburg. 'What are they saying?'

Natalie scowled, looking almost as angry as Loren felt at that moment. 'Everyone is very curious to know how you and the chief kept yourselves occupied during those four hours you were trapped together, and you can imagine how their evil little minds are working overtime.'

'Oh, lord!' Loren groaned, a thread of anxiety winding its way through her. 'I wonder if these rumours have reached Mr Beaumont's ears.'

'I bet they have,' Natalie laughed mirthlessly.

'It's rather like piling disaster upon disaster, isn't it?'
Loren's smile was acid. 'First I nearly lose him a
contract, then I spill hot coffee all over him, and finally
I set the tongues wagging by getting myself closeted in a
lift with him!'

'You're not angry with me for telling you, are you?

'I'm not angry with you,' Loren assured her hastily,
but her mouth tightened as comprehension dawned.
'Now I know, at least, why everyone has been eyeing
me so oddly all morning.'

They drank their tea and left the canteen, and Loren
had barely sat down behind her desk when Harvey
Griffin summoned her into his office.

'Miss Fraser . . .' He shuffled the papers unnecessarily
on the desk, but he did not look up at Loren who stood
facing him quietly. 'About last night.'

'Yes, Mr Griffin?' said Loren, her voice cool despite
her rising anger at what she felt was downright
curiosity.

'I presume you took that report up to Mr
MacDonald's office, and it was when you were leaving
that the unfortunate incident occurred?'

'Yes, Mr Griffin.'

He looked up then, and she could almost feel sorry
for him when she sensed his discomfort. 'What
happened, Miss Fraser?'

'I presume you mean what happened while we were
trapped in the lift?' she queried with a wry smile, and a
dull red stain stood out on his cheeks.

'That's correct.' He looked up once again, saw her
hesitate, and said hastily, 'For Mr Beaumont's sake,
and for yours, these rumours must be squashed, and I
can't help unless I know the truth.'

'Nothing happened, Mr Griffin,' Loren told him, her
voice cool with suppressed anger. 'We sat on the floor
and talked to pass the time. I told him a bit about

myself, and he reciprocated in a similar manner. We shared my half a slab of chocolate and his small flask of brandy when we realised we were hungry, and then we talked some more until the technicians set us free.'

Harvey Griffin studied her intently through the thick lenses of his spectacles. 'Was that all?'

'What did you expect, Griffin? A sordid tale of lust in the lift?' Steve Beaumont's deep-throated voice demanded harshly from the doorway, and Loren felt her cheeks stinging as she swung round in alarm to face him.

'Mr Beaumont, sir.' Harvey Griffin almost choked on the words as he shot up behind his desk to face the man who had entered his office so silently. 'I was merely questioning Miss Fraser in the hope of bringing to an end the unseemly rumours concerning yourself and this young lady.'

Steve Beaumont's eyes were like chips of ice in his deeply tanned face, and Loren felt chilled into her marrow. 'I appreciate that, Griffin,' he acknowledged in a clipped voice, and Loren found herself ushered towards the interleading door. 'Now, if you'll excuse me, I'd like a private word with Miss Fraser.'

Harvey Griffin spluttered an embarrassed reply, but Loren was already preceding Steve Beaumont into her office, and he closed the door firmly behind them before he turned to face her.

He did not speak for a moment, and the atmosphere was loaded with tension. He looked grim about the mouth, but his keen glance did not miss the nervous flutter of her hands before she clasped them tightly in front of her.

'Last night in the lift you said you felt as if you owed me an apology,' he said eventually, 'and that's exactly how I feel now.'

'I doubt if it will help, if you'll forgive me quoting

you, Mr Beaumont,' she smiled faintly, wondering if
Harvey Griffin had nerve enough to stand with his ear
glued to the keyhole.

Steve Beaumont's mouth curved in a semblance of a
smile. 'I hope you haven't been upset or hurt by these
unkind rumours?'

'My conscience is clear.' She met his gaze unfalter-
ingly, then she exploded in a spurt of agitation. 'For
heaven's sake, Mr Beaumont, nothing happened that
either you or I have to be ashamed of!'

'Your attitude is commendable,' he observed, his
smile deepening with a hint of mockery. 'You've no
doubt had to deal with these sort of rumours before?'

Loren did not know whether to laugh or to be angry,
but she slowly regained her composure, and her voice
was calm when she spoke. 'In a small community like
Aberdeen a rumour will spread as fast as whirling dust
across the plains, but it seldom lasts longer than it takes
for the dust to settle, and tomorrow they'll find
something else to talk about.'

'You're right, of course,' he agreed abruptly, turning
towards the door. 'I won't keep you from your work.'

'Mr Beaumont ...' He turned, his eyes cool and
distant when they met hers, and her smile faltered.
'Thanks for the meal you had sent to my flat last night.'

He inclined his head briefly and walked out of her
office, but she was left feeling faintly breathless and
curious. He could be so vibrantly male that her senses
would be aroused by merely looking at him, yet just as
swiftly he could freeze her by slipping into the role of
the cool and distant chief of Beaumont Engineering.

Loren did not know which she preferred, but she
decided at length that she would be happier if she
managed to stay out of his way in future. He was far
too disturbing for her own peace of mind, and she was
aware of the physical awareness he had awakened in her

from the first moment she had set eyes on him. She had learned something about Steve Beaumont which was well worth remembering. He lived by his own code of morals, and they most certainly did not match her own. They had been thrown together for a few hours under unusual circumstances, but there was no earthly reason why they should meet again unless it was absolutely necessary. It amazed her, however, that he should have felt the need to apologise to her for the wild speculations which their forced internment in the lift had aroused—but then, she supposed, she would never quite understand a man like Steve Beaumont.

CHAPTER FOUR

As Loren had predicted, the rumours and speculations died a swift and natural death, and they did so without the well-intended assistance of Harvey Griffin. Everything seemed to settle down to normality, and she hoped it would stay that way, but her hopes were shattered when she arrived at her office one morning two weeks later. She removed the cover of her typewriter, and there, held firmly under the paper bail, was an envelope addressed to her. She recognised that bold, masculine handwriting at once, and hastily removed the envelope to thrust it into her desk drawer before anyone could see it. Her heart was pounding against her ribs, and her mouth felt strangely dry. It was almost as if she had done something which she ought to feel guilty about, and she hated Steve Beaumont at that moment for making her feel this way.

Harvey Griffin called her into his office to take down dictation, and it was after ten that morning before she had an opportunity to open the envelope and read its contents. Steve Beaumont had used paper from the personal notepad on her desk, and it gave her the oddest feeling to think that he had perhaps sat in her chair to write this note which was written in a similar vein to the one she had received with the meal he had had sent up to her flat.

To disprove my theory that we can only meet in disastrous circumstances I've booked a table for us this evening at a quiet little restaurant. Be ready at seven. S.B.

Loren crushed the note in her hand as she leaned back in her chair and tried to remain calm despite the anger which was beginning to pulse through her. The audacity of the man! How *dared* he simply take it for granted that she would have dinner with him that evening? He might not know it, but she had a mind of her own, and he was going to receive a firm refusal.

She dialled his office number on the internal telephone, and moments later Mrs Markham's voice said crisply into her ear. 'Mr Beaumont's office, can I help you?'

'I'd like to speak to Mr Beaumont, please,' Loren replied in an equally crisp voice.

'Who am I speaking to?'

'Loren Fraser from the Accounts department.'

A momentary silence followed this disclosure, and there was a distinct chill of displeasure in Mrs Markham's voice when she said: 'I'm afraid Mr Beaumont is chairing a directors' meeting. Would you like to leave a message?'

Loren had been fuming, ready to do battle, but quite suddenly she felt like a deflated balloon. 'No, I—I'll call again later.'

'As you wish.'

The line went dead with a decisive crackle that jarred in Loren's ear, and she replaced the receiver with equal force. *'Damn!'*

'Tut-tut! What language, Miss Fraser, and on such a beautiful morning,' Natalie rebuked her humorously as she entered Loren's office and perched herself in a familiar manner on the corner of the desk. 'Has something happened to upset you?'

'Oh ... it's nothing,' Loren tried to brush aside her query, but the dark-eyed girl seated on her desk would not be put off that easily.

'Come on, you can tell Aunty Natalie.'

'You're simply inquisitive,' Loren accused with a wry smile.

'I admit it, but you know my lips are always sealed, and you know it helps to talk,' Natalie grinned impishly. 'Come on . . . tell me all.'

Natalie was not a gossip, that much was true, but she was persistent, and Loren finally voiced the reason for her annoyance.

'I've received an invitation from Mr Beaumont to have dinner with him this evening.' Loren pulled a face and added: 'Invitation isn't exactly the right word, it was more like an order.'

'You must have made quite an impression on him,' Natalie laughed softly with an amusement Loren could not echo. 'Are you going to accept his invitation?'

'I'm going to refuse it,' Loren stated flatly, her brow creasing with annoyance. 'I tried to speak to him on the telephone, but Mrs Markham told me he was chairing a directors' meeting.'

Natalie's eyes widened in disbelief as she studied Loren closely. 'Are you serious about refusing to go out with him?'

'Natalie, I . . .' Loren paused abruptly, incapable of explaining even to herself why she wished to decline Steve Beaumont's invitation, and she grasped at the first thing that came to mind. 'It never pays to become involved with one's employer.'

'I agree,' Natalie nodded solemnly, 'but Steve Beaumont is really dishy, and I'd say "yes" like a shot if he invited me to dine with him.'

'Oh, Natalie,' Loren laughed helplessly, 'he scares me to death!'

'He scares me too, but I like being scared,' Natalie confessed with an impish grin on her face and a pretended shiver of ecstasy, and Loren was still laughing softly to herself long after Natalie had left her office.

She tried to contact Steve Beaumont once again that

afternoon, but this time she was told that he was out, and that he would not be returning to his office. That left her with no alternative but to be ready at seven as he had instructed in his note, and the mere thought of it made her fume inwardly once again.

Loren went home that afternoon, and she felt nothing but dread for the evening ahead of her as she bathed and changed into something suitable. The cinnamon-coloured dress with its long sleeves was perfect for Johannesburg's chilly nights as winter settled on the Reef, and the plain, flowing style of the dress gave her that much needed look of confidence. She pinned up her hair to hide her nervousness behind that look of elegance and sophistication which she felt she did not possess, but she used her make-up sparingly as usual. She had naturally healthy skin, for which she was grateful, and she had managed to keep it healthy with very little care. Her eyes stared back at her quite steadily in the dressing table mirror, but they were sparkling with the anger she had laboured under most of the day. Steve Beaumont might have manipulated her into dining with him this evening, but she was going to make her displeasure known regardless of his exalted position in Beaumont Engineering.

The doorbell chimed at precisely seven o'clock, but instead of speaking her mind when she let him in, she found herself staring at him a little stupidly. He looked devastatingly handsome in a dark evening suit, and she felt her anger melt away as if it had never existed.

'Ready?' he asked abruptly, but she saw a faint smile curving his perfectly chiselled mouth, and those incredibly blue eyes were sliding over her with appreciation mirrored in their depths.

'Yes, I'm ready,' she said quickly, turning from him to collect her wrap and evening purse where she had left them on a chair in the lounge.

'It's a miracle,' Steve Beaumont remarked with a hint of mockery in his voice when she had locked the door and they were walking towards the lift. 'I haven't yet met a woman who could be ready at the stipulated time.'

'You've met one now,' she replied stiffly, determined not to be swayed by that fatal magnetism which was casting a spell on her.

The lift doors slid open, and when they stepped into it Loren could not help recalling those hours they had been trapped together in a similarly confined space. Steve Beaumont was thinking about that incident as well, she could see it in the vaguely sardonic gleam that lit his eyes when he glanced at her, but neither of them spoke as the lift bore them safely down to the ground floor.

The tomato red Jaguar was parked at the entrance and, despite her anger, Loren found herself admiring the luxurious interior. The cushioned seats had been created for supreme comfort, and warm air flowed from the air-conditioner to make travelling on a cold night a pleasure instead of an ordeal, but Loren did not thaw sufficiently to speak to the man beside her in anything but a cool, polite tone.

The Italian restaurant where Steve had booked a table was small and intimate. The lights were dim along the wood-panelled walls, and candles flickered and smoked on small tables covered with red checkered cloths. The atmosphere was unmistakably continental, and so was the elaborate menu, but Steve Beaumont ordered a bottle of their best wine to be brought to the table while they studied the menu. The restaurant was reasonably full with people coming and going, but Loren barely noticed while she tried to decipher the menu, and she finally gave up the effort, leaving it to Steve Beaumont to order for her after their wine had been poured.

'You seem to be annoyed with me for some reason,' he smiled mockingly, and she had a feeling that he had known exactly how she would react to his arrogant and unexpected invitation.

'I am annoyed,' Loren confessed without hesitation, her eyes meeting his across the candlelit table. 'Your invitation was an arrogant supposition that I would be free this evening to dine with you, and I don't very much care for such tactics.'

'You could have declined,' he pointed out with a casualness that made her suspect that he could not care less whether she had suffered any inconvenience.

'I tried to contact you, but first you were at a directors' meeting, and then you were out.' Her eyes sparked yellow fire at him across the table. 'What would have happened if I'd had another engagement lined up for this evening?'

'You would have had to cancel it.'

She stared at him, momentarily speechless. He had spoken without any real emphasis, but she knew that he had meant every word. 'Are you always this arrogant, Mr Beaumont?'

'It usually helps me get what I want.' He lit a cigarette and studied her with narrowed eyes through a haze of smoke. 'Why didn't you want to have dinner with me?'

'I don't believe in mixing business with pleasure.'

A mocking smile curved his mouth. 'Correct me if I'm wrong, but isn't that exactly what you did with your former employer.'

'Matt Kruger was different,' Loren argued, taking a sip of wine to steady herself as she attempted to wriggle herself out of that proverbial tight corner.

'How different?' Steve Beaumont demanded abruptly.

'He was neither pushy nor arrogant.'

'He must have been a bore.'

His mocking smile had deepened, and she could almost feel her blood pressure rise by several degrees. 'If you're trying to annoy me, Mr Beaumont, then you're succeeding admirably.'

'I've developed quite a phobia about you, Loren Fraser, and I don't particularly care for phobias.' He sat forward, leaning his elbows on the table so that the flame of the candle accentated the hollows and planes of his ruggedly handsome features. 'I had a feeling you might refuse my invitation to dine with me this evening, and that's the reason why I was determined not to give you the opportunity to decline.'

'You consider this evening as some sort of experiment?' she asked after pausing a moment for thought.

'Not entirely.' His mouth curved sensuously, and her pulse quickened in alarm when he lowered his eyes to observe the agitated rise and fall of her breasts beneath the soft material of her dress. 'You're a very lovely woman, Loren, and I enjoy your company to the extent that I want to get to know you a lot better.'

Loren shivered inwardly. This man frightened her for some reason, but she could not find an explanation for her fears. Perhaps he was too aggressively male, or perhaps it was her own response to his masculinity which disturbed her most.

'I'm nothing but a raw country girl, Mr Beaumont, and I doubt if you'll find me interesting for very long,' she pointed out drily.

'That's a chance I'm willing to take.'

She felt as if she were being edged into a corner, and it was a feeling she disliked intensely. 'Mr Beaumont, I——'

'Steve,' he interrupted smoothly. 'Call me Steve.'

'Steve,' she conceded, but she was determined not to

give another inch. 'You must know plenty of women who would suit you far better than I ever would.'

Smoke curled from his nostrils, giving him a devilish appearance, and his eyes held hers mockingly through the smoky haze. 'At the moment I'm between women.'

'I refuse to act as a diversion,' she retorted stiffly.

'I don't consider you a diversion, Loren,' he contradicted, putting out his cigarette and draining his glass of wine. 'I consider you a challenge.'

'A challenge?' she questioned, instantly on her guard.

'A raw country girl who's never gone to bed with a man before is quite a challenge.' He smiled cynically. 'Wouldn't you say so?'

'Are you generalising, or is this your subtle way of letting me know that some time in the future you intend to persuade me into your bed?' she asked, matching cynicism with cynicism.

'Does the thought excite you?'

'To be quite frank, it amuses me.'

His eyebrows rose sharply, and he paused in the process of filling up their glasses. 'May I know why you find it amusing?'

'Well, it's either that, or slapping your face.' Her eyes sparkled with sudden humour as they met his. 'Which would you prefer?'

Steve topped up their glasses and cast a swift glance across the crowded restaurant before he met her steady gaze with a hint of sardonic humour in his blue eyes. 'I think the amusement will do for now.'

'I knew you'd agree with me,' she smiled sweetly, and he raised his glass of wine to toast her.

'You're the most refreshing woman I've met in a long time.'

Loren did not reply to that and, when their meal was served, she succeeded in keeping the conversation centred for a while on the superbly prepared Italian dishes. Steve had travelled extensively in his life, and he later enthralled her with snippets of information and little anecdotes about things which had occurred in the various countries he had visited, but when their coffee was served the conversation once again veered in a personal direction.

'Are you an only child, Loren, or do you have a brother tucked away somewhere to carry on the family tradition of sheep farming?' he questioned her without his usual mockery.

'I'm an only child,' she told him gravely. 'When I was two my mother lost the baby she was carrying, and after that she couldn't have children again.'

'What will happen to the farm?'

'I'll inherit it, I suppose,' she replied, sipping at the hot, aromatic coffee, and realising that this was something she had not give much thought to in the past.

'Is that what you want to do?' he asked incredulously. 'Bury yourself on a sheep farm?'

'That will depend on the future. I might want to give it a bash on my own, or I might install a manager to take care of the farm for me, but it's not something I want to think of just yet.' She slid an idle finger along the rim of her cup and decided it was time to swing the subject away from her. 'What about yourself? Any brothers or sisters?'

'I have a younger brother who emigrated to Australia some years ago,' Steve told her, lighting a cigarette and blowing a stream of smoke towards the beamed ceiling. 'He's a neuro-surgeon, and I believe he's doing well for himself.'

'Is he married?' she asked before she could prevent herself.

'He married an Australian girl, and they have two children.' Cynicism curved his sensuous mouth and glittered in his eyes. 'The poor fellow was crazy enough to fall madly in love ... whatever that may be. Now he's stuck with one woman for life, and kids to support.'

Loren felt something tighten in her chest. 'You obviously don't believe in love.'

'You might as well ask me if I believe in ghosts,' Steve laughed shortly, drawing hard on his cigarette. 'Until I encounter it I will continue to view it with scepticism.'

She did not pursue the subject, and neither did Steve, but Loren had discovered something else about Steve Beaumont which did not somehow appeal to her. He did not want the bondage of marriage, and he did not believe in love. The latter would also, no doubt, interfere with his desire for freedom, and she could only pity the unfortunate woman who would ever be foolish enough to fall in love with him.

They left the restaurant a few minutes later and walked out into the cold night to where he had parked his Jaguar. Loren shivered, but the air-conditioner swiftly warmed the interior of the car, and she found herself thinking she was glad that the evening was almost at an end.

'Well, we've survived the evening without a major or minor disaster occurring,' Steve remarked almost as if he had read her thoughts partially, and Loren was about to agree with him when the Jaguar's engine spluttered and came to a jerking halt in the side lane of the busy, well-lit street. 'It seems I spoke too soon,' Steve groaned.

'Do you keep a torch somewhere?' she asked as he reached beneath the dashboard to tug at the lever for opening the bonnet.

'In the glove compartment.'

Loren found the torch and got out of the car to walk

round to the front. She raised the bonnet and, in the
beam of the torch light, swiftly acquainted herself with
the engine, so that when Steve joined her there she had
already detected the fault.

'The low tension wire from the coil to the distributor
has worked itself loose,' she told him, lighting with the
torch directly on the spot she was speaking of.

'Clever girl,' he murmured as he reconnected the
wire, then he lowered the bonnet and secured it safely
before they returned to the warm interior of the car.
'You're beginning to intrigue me, Loren Fraser,' he told
her, wiping his hands on a spotlessly white handkerchief,
and turning the key in the ignition.

'Because I know something about a car's engine?' she
asked as the Jaguar purred to life beneath her.

'Among other things, yes,' he smiled faintly as he
manoeuvred the Jaguar into the steady stream of late
night traffic.

'I grew up on a farm, remember, and I learnt to do
everything from shearing a sheep to overhauling the
engine of a truck,' she reminded him with a hint of
mockery in her voice.

'Your father must have wanted a son badly.'

Loren laughed at the ridiculous suggestion. 'My
father would have been quite happy if I'd stayed at
home and played with my dolls, but instead I followed
him around like a second shadow, and I often think he
must have taught me everything I know simply to get
me out of his hair *and* his way.'

Steve was silent for a time, but a faintly mocking
smile played about his mouth when he glanced at her
briefly. 'Would you call this incident a disaster?'

'If you're referring to the loosened wire, then no, I
wouldn't call it that.'

'Our evening so far is still disaster-free, then?'

Loren took care in hiding her smile. 'Absolutely.'

'Good!' he remarked with such a wealth of satisfaction that she almost laughed out loud, but she stopped herself just in time.

The cushioned seat was so comfortable, and the hum of the engine so soothing, that Loren almost fell asleep during the remainder of the short distance to her flat.

'Well, we made it,' Steve remarked, parking his car at the entrance to the building, and undoing his seat-belt before he turned to face her.

'We made it,' she echoed, rousing herself, and fumbling in the darkness with her own seat-belt.

He helped her with the catch, but their hands somehow became entangled and, when the belt snapped loose, he had her right hand trapped between both of his. The fiery warmth of his mouth brushed briefly against the inside of her wrist before shifting to her palm, and there was something so acutely intimate about this casual caress that her breath locked momentarily in her throat as she felt an almost electrifying, wholly pleasurable sensation rippling up her arm. He leaned towards her, her name a low growl deep in his throat, and she came sharply to her senses.

Snatching her hand from his, she tore open the door beside her. 'Goodnight, Mr Beaumont, and thank you for a pleasant evening.'

She was out of the car before he could prevent her, but Steve moved with incredible speed, and he was there beside her when she stepped into the lift. Her heart was beating like a sledge-hammer against her breastbone, and she felt certain he could hear it as he stood beside her in the lift which swept them up to the ninth floor. He did not say anything, and she did not risk glancing at him. She was too confused even to think straight, and she stared fixedly at the carpet beneath her feet until the lift doors slid open again.

'Are you inviting me in for coffee?' he asked, breaking the stony silence between them when she inserted the key into the lock.

'No, I'm not,' she announced, not caring how rude it might sound, but he forced his way into the flat the moment the door swung open beneath her hand, and her angry eyes flashed yellow fire up at him when she discarded her wrap and purse. 'I said *no!*'

Steve kicked the door shut and gripped her shoulders so tightly that a numb pain shot down the length of her arms into her hands. 'Stop it, Loren! Stop behaving like a petrified virgin!'

A petrified virgin! That shocked her back to normality where everything else might have failed, and she reluctantly admitted to herself that she was exactly that; a petrified virgin in the face of Steve Beaumont's raw, animal masculinity. In a moment of blind panic she had lost her composure, her only defence, and that was something she would have to watch in future.

'Your experiment has been a success, Mr Beaumont,' she said coolly, brushing off his hands and putting a safe distance between them. 'Nothing disastrous has occurred, but don't trust your luck too far.'

His mouth tightened. 'You're determined to keep me at arm's length, is that it?'

'I'm quite determined that any future meetings will be confined strictly to the offices of Beaumont Engineering.'

'Why?' he rapped out the question, his eyes burning down into hers, and making it difficult for her to sustain his glance.

'I believe I told you earlier that I don't intend to act as a diversion while you're between women.'

'Dammit, I don't want you as a diversion!' he argued, his deep-throated voice so harsh that it grated along her taut nerves.

'What is expected of me, then?' she asked, maintaining her outwardly cool appearance with difficulty. 'Do you expect me to willingly step in where the last woman has left off?'

His head shot up a fraction, and a gleam of derision lurked in his eyes. 'I don't expect you will do anything *willingly* at the moment, but the truth is . . .' He paused and raised a hand as if to touch her, but she backed a pace away from him, and he smiled twistedly as he let his hand fall to his side again. 'I've always made a rule of not involving myself with a virgin, but I want you, Loren.'

She felt the blood drain away from her face, then it rushed back again with a force that stung her cheeks. She was a woman of twenty-five, and she had often prided herself on her ability to cope with any emergency, but she had never imagined she would ever find herself faced with something quite like this. In Aberdeen no self-respecting man would have voiced his desire for a woman quite so bluntly, but this was not Aberdeen, and Steve Beaumont was a man quite unlike any other man she had ever met in her life.

There was only one way to react to his blunt statement, she decided eventually, and that was to be equally blunt in her refusal. 'I'm sorry, Mr Beaumont, but I'm not on the market as an object to satisfy your sex drive, so I suggest you look elsewhere for that type of merchandise.'

His jaw hardened and his eyes darkened with fury as he bridged the gap between them in two long strides. He had moved so swiftly that there had been no time to evade those outstretched hands, and she was jerked against him with a force that momentarily knocked the breath from her body.

'I was being honest with you, but I'm damned if I'll stand here and take your insults!' he announced savagely, and she had a distorted vision of his ruggedly

handsome features before his hard mouth settled on
hers.

The unexpected contact with his male body had given
her resistance its first crumbling blow, but the touch of
his lips against her own could have led to ruin if she
had not clung to her sanity so desperately. Heart
pounding and senses roaring, she placed her hands flat
against his wide chest, and she somehow managed to
thrust him from her.

'How dare you!' she cried in a choked voice, her hand
swinging back of its own volition to strike him, but he
caught her wrist smartly in the air and twisted her arm
behind her back as he pulled her roughly into his arms
again.

Devilish laughter, low and throaty, passed his lips,
skimming across her quivering nerves, and for the first
time in her life she knew what it felt like to be almost
paralysed with fear. She tried to avoid his descending
mouth, but his hand was in her hair, scattering the pins
and forcing her to hold her head still unless she wanted
to inflict pain on herself. He laughed again, and he
sounded more like the devil than before. He was
obviously enjoying her helplessness, and she hated him
when he lowered his head to tantalise her lips with
feather-light kisses.

Steve Beaumont was an expert at getting what he
wanted. Loren realised this in those final moments
before her tight rein on her emotions snapped, and they
went soaring out of control. She could feel his heart
beating as wildly as her own when he curved her now
pliant body into his, and in the far recesses of her mind
she felt ashamed of herself, but she was unable to
control her lips from parting and moving beneath his.
He was as aware of her response as she was of his
physical need, she could see it in his mocking eyes when
he raised his head for a moment, and she trembled

when his warm mouth shifted over hers again, parting her lips and invading her mouth with an intimacy that sent an alien fire darting through her veins.

His hands slid down her back, moulding her even closer to him until it felt as if he were grinding his hips into hers, and when he finally released her she found that she was trembling so much that she had to cling to the lapels of his jacket to steady herself. She felt dazed and incapable of standing on legs that felt like jelly beneath her, but her sanity returned swiftly and brought with it a stinging humiliation which made her relinquish her hold on him to lean weakly against the high-backed chair close to her.

'You're not as cold as ice after all, Loren Fraser,' Steve mocked her ruthlessly. 'I believe that under that cool and confident exterior there lurks a passionate woman seeking an outlet, and, when you're ready, I'll be here to provide it!'

He walked out of the flat, and her eyes followed him as if drawn by a magnet until the door closed behind his tall, wide-shouldered frame. Shame washed over her like a heated tide as his words penetrated her mind with a searing stab. He had proved, to himself *and* to her, that she was a woman like any other, and that she was capable of feeling emotions she had not even known existed.

She moved automatically, picking up the pins which had been ripped from her hair and locking the door securely, but when she reached the bedroom she fell across the bed with a moan on her lips. She was ashamed of the way she had behaved, and of the encouragement she had given without actually intending to. Worst of all, she had no idea how she was going to face Steve Beaumont again in future.

'I believe that under that cool and confident exterior there lurks a passionate woman seeking an outlet, and, when you're ready, I'll be here to provide it,' his words reverberated through her mind.

It had sounded like a threat, and she dared not ignore it. He was capable of making her feel and do things which were quite alien to her, and no other man had ever succeeded in making her lose control in such a shameful way before. Steve Beaumont held an attraction for her which she could not deny. She had been aware of it that very first time she had seen him, and it had grown stronger with every meeting. She despised him for what he was, and she would go on despising him, but unfortunately that made no difference to the way her body reacted to his presence. He was a disruptive force against which she would have to be on her guard, but heaven only knew how she would cope if he persisted in breaking her down physically and emotionally. Common sense warned her that she would end up like malleable clay in his expert hands, but common sense would be no help to her at all if she had to find herself in a similar situation to the one she had found herself in this evening. He was accustomed to getting his own way, and she had a horrible feeling that, where women were concerned, his methods were not always completely fair. Perhaps he was used to women falling all over themselves for his attention, but she was determined that he was not going to have it that easy with her.

Loren took off her clothes and put on her nightdress, and by the time she had removed her make-up she felt considerably calmer, but, for the first time since arriving in Johannesburg, she found herself doubting her decision to leave her familiar surroundings. It had perhaps been a mistake, but she was not going to give up that easily.

The telephone rang, and Loren frowned at the alarm on the bedside cupboard. Who could be calling her at eleven o'clock in the evening? Steve Beaumont? Fear made her decide not to answer it, but then she realised that it could also be her parents, and it was this thought that sent her flying into the lounge. She missed them dreadfully at that moment, but, when she lifted the receiver and gave her number, the voice at the other end did not belong to her mother or her father. It was Natalie, and she sounded vaguely distressed.

'I called earlier this evening, but there was no reply, and I've been rather worried about you,' she said, and then she asked pointedly, 'Has he gone? Is everything all right?'

'Everything is all right. Mr Beaumont left an hour ago, and I'm on my way to bed.'

'Oh . . . sorry,' Natalie apologised hastily. 'We'll talk in the morning.'

'Natalie,' Loren said quickly before she could ring off, 'I appreciate your concern.'

'I always worry about the people I care about,' Natalie laughed selfconsciously. 'Goodnight, Loren.'

The line went dead, and Loren felt considerably better after that brief conversation with Natalie Miller. Natalie had disproved her parents' theory. People do still care about each other in a city the size of Johannesburg, and that was a comforting thought to take to bed with her.

CHAPTER FIVE

'WHAT happened last night?' Natalie questioned Loren with inquisitive concern during the course of the morning.

'Nothing happened which I wasn't able to cope with,' Loren told what she considered the biggest lie this century, and crossed her fingers childishly under the desk.

'Are you going to see him again? On a date, I mean?'

'Not if I can help it!' Loren was adamant, but deep down she had a gnawing suspicion that Steve Beaumont was not easily discouraged.

'Well, you won't be seeing him this week anyway,' Natalie set her mind at rest temporarily. 'I hear the big chief is off this morning on a flight to Namibia and I believe he won't be back until next week Friday.'

'Quite honestly, Natalie, I'm not interested in what he does and where he goes,' Loren protested, but that was not quite true. Knowing that he would be gone for at least a week filled her with intense relief at the thought of not having to face him quite so soon after last night.

Natalie eyed Loren speculatively. 'In other words, you couldn't care less about him just as long as he stays out of your way?'

'Exactly!'

'Boy, he must have come on heavy last night!'

'Come on heavy?' Loren queried blankly.

'I mean he made a pass at you, and you didn't like it.'

Loren managed to control her expression with difficulty. Natalie was much too astute for comfort, and she glanced at her sternly. 'Haven't you got any work to do?'

'I'm going,' Natalie grinned, but before she reached the door she turned to add with mock sobriety, 'You ought to feel flattered, you know. The big chief has never looked twice at any woman in this building before.'

'I'm flattered, but I'm not interested,' Loren insisted firmly. 'Satisfied?'

Mischief danced in Natalie's eyes. 'For the moment, yes.'

She closed the door behind her and, for the first time, Loren allowed her facial muscles to relax. If Natalie could have seen her then she would have seen a frightened woman stripped of her confidence. Steve Beaumont had become a threat to her very existence, and she was not flattered by Natalie's teasing remark. The thought that Steve had never looked twice at another woman in the building left her feeling more afraid than before.

Knowing that Steve was away for a week in Namibia helped to some extent. Her nerves unravelled themselves into their proper order, and she was able to concentrate fully on her work, but she knew that it would not last. He would be back, and her confidence in herself had been dealt a blow so severe that she actually feared their next meeting.

During the course of the following week she opened her door early one evening to find Matt Kruger standing on her doorstep. Tall and lean, with his dark hair curling characteristically on to his forehead, he smiled down into her surprised eyes.

'How absolutely wonderful to see you!' she exclaimed, extending both hands and drawing him in out of the cold.

'I hope you don't mind my dropping in unexpectedly like this, but I'm on my way to the northern Transvaal for a few days, and I thought I'd stop over for the night to find out how you are.'

'Is this a holiday trip, or business?' she asked as she led him into the lounge.

'Holiday,' he smiled, his clear grey eyes creasing at the corners.

'About time too,' she retorted when she thought of how little time he took off from his practice.

'Your parents told me to say they send their love,' Matt informed her when he had lowered his lean length into a comfortable chair.

'You saw them?'

'I was out on the farm for a brief visit before I left Aberdeen.' His expression sobered as he stretched out his long legs. 'Your father hasn't been too well lately.'

'Oh, no!' Loren exclaimed, her face paling.

'It's nothing serious,' Matt reassured her. 'It's his old back injury, and Aberdeen is experiencing one of its worst winters.'

'I've spoken to my parents on the telephone several times, but my father never said a word about not being well,' Loren frowned.

'What your father really needs is someone to help him on the farm,' Matt put his finger on the pulse of the problem, and a wry smile curved her mouth.

'I've had quite an argument with him about that, but he's too stubborn to admit that he can no longer manage it all on his own.'

'Come and have dinner somewhere with me?' Matt changed the subject, his gravelly voice falling with a pleasant familiarity on her ears.

'I have a better idea,' she smiled. 'Why don't you stay here and have dinner with me?'

He seemed to hesitate. 'I'd like that, but only if you're sure it's not too much trouble.'

'Sit there and relax,' she ordered firmly. 'If you'd like to pour yourself a glass of wine you'll find a bottle and glasses in that walnut cabinet next to the hi-fi.'

She left him in the lounge while she went into the kitchen. She opened the refrigerator and searched for something which was quick to prepare. There was fillet steak, and the salad she had prepared before Matt had arrived. To add to that she could bake a few potatoes, and open a tin of peas.

'I don't like drinking on my own,' Matt smiled at her some minutes later when he strolled into the kitchen and placed a glass of wine on the table close to her.

'Thanks,' she smiled back at him, raising her glass. 'Here's to your brief holiday.'

Their eyes met and held over the rim of their glasses as they sipped their wine, but there was nothing intimate about the way they looked at each other. It was, on both sides, merely a silent appraisal of an old and trusted friend.

'I like your flat,' Matt remarked at length, glancing about him appreciatively.

'It isn't mine, actually,' Loren explained, putting the potatoes in the oven and closing the oven door. 'It belongs to the sister and brother-in-law of a girl I work with, and I'm merely staying here to look after the place until they return from their overseas trip.'

'So you're still looking for a place of your own?'

'Yes, but without much success so far,' she grimaced.

'I'm pretty good at grilling a steak, if you'd care to let me help you,' Matt offered, and Loren left him to it while she took out plates and laid the table.

It was strange to have Matt there in the kitchen with her. Being a bachelor, he was quite domesticated, but she imagined he would hate it if she had to tell him so. In all the years she had worked for him she had never believed she would see him in this role, and it was difficult to believe that this was the man who could be so utterly harsh and ruthless in a courtroom.

Matt was good at grilling steak, as he had said, and

she complimented him on his expertise when they finally sat down to eat the meal they had prepared together. There were no awkward moments, and they found a lot to talk about. They were reminiscing mostly about the past, and laughing about amusing incidents which had occurred during the four years she had been his secretary. Loren was relaxed and totally at ease with this man, and she could not help thinking how different it was when she was with Steve Beaumont. With Steve she was tense, always on her guard, and constantly aware of a disturbing undercurrent to everything which was said between them.

She tried to shrug him off mentally, but she did not succeed entirely, and Matt was quick to notice that something was wrong when they had washed the dishes and were returning to the lounge with the tray of coffee.

'Do you like your job?' he questioned her.

'It's not quite the same as working for you, but the pay is good,' she confessed with a rueful smile.

'Meaning that I didn't pay you enough?' he teased her, but his eyes were watchful.

'Meaning that some days I'm convinced it's the pay cheque alone that makes me stay on here,' she sighed, and his glance sharpened.

'Why don't you come home to Aberdeen if you're not happy?'

'Oh, I'm happy enough.'

'But?' Matt prompted, still observing her closely.

'But nothing,' she smiled stiffly. 'I miss my home, but I'm happy enough in what I'm doing.'

His keen glance did not waver, and it made her feel vaguely uncomfortable. He knew her too well, and he saw too much. 'I think something has happened; something serious, and you don't want to talk about it.'

'What makes you think that something has

happened?' she asked, veiling her eyes, and exercising a rigid control on her features.

'I know you too well,' he confirmed her suspicions. 'And attorneys like myself are sometimes quite adept at reading between the lines.'

'Now, let me see . . . you like your coffee strong with a dash of milk and plenty of sugar,' Loren deliberately evaded his probing questions as she leaned forward to prepare his coffee the way he liked it. 'I'm surprised you've never put on weight, considering the amount of sugar you take in your tea and coffee.'

'You're changing the subject,' he accused as she handed him his cup.

'I don't want to talk about myself. I would rather talk about you, and about Aberdeen, and——'

'Loren!' he interrupted her sharply. 'What are you afraid of?'

'Don't, Matt,' she pleaded, gesturing with her hands and wishing she could physically ward off his probing queries.

'I don't want to pry, but you know you can trust me, and if you're in some kind of trouble, then I'd like to help you,' he said gravely. 'I mean that, Loren.'

'I know you do.' She swallowed down the lump in her throat. 'But I'm not in any kind of trouble, not yet anyway.'

They drank their coffee in silence, but she felt his eyes resting on her, and she knew he was far from satisfied with the outcome of his friendly interrogation.

'I believe Beaumont Engineering is a company belonging to a man of the same name,' Matt steered the conversation in a different direction, but the topic he chose did not diminish her wariness,

'That's correct,' she answered carefully. 'His name is Steve Beaumont,'

'Have you met him?'

'Yes, we've bumped into each other a few times.' Her voice sounded calm and even, and she congratulated herself silently.

'What's he like?'

'I haven't had much to do with him, so I can't really say,' she replied evasively. 'My boss in the Accounts department is Harvey Griffin.'

'Old or young?' Matt asked with a teasing smile.

'Middle-aged,' she laughed, relaxing her guard as they stepped on to safer ground. 'He's a genius with figures, he has an odd sense of humour, and although he means well, he can be terribly tactless at times.'

'He sounds like one of my old university professors,' Matt laughed. 'The man was a walking encyclopaedia of law, but in private he always seemed to say the wrong thing.'

'Harvey Griffin is a very nice man, actually,' Loren felt compelled to add in her boss's defence.

'He's a very lucky man to have you working for him,' Matt said enviously, glancing at his wrist watch and getting up reluctantly. 'I'm afraid I must get back to the hotel.'

'So early?' she protested, unable to hide her disappointment.

'I have a long stretch ahead of me tomorrow, and I'll have to have an early night if I want to leave at five in the morning,' he smiled ruefully.

'I'm very glad you could spare the time to come and see me,' she said quite sincerely as she accompanied him to the door, and, for the first time since knowing him, he kissed her lightly on the lips instead of the cheek.

'I've missed you,' he told her, and then he was gone.

Loren closed the door and leaned against it for a moment. Now that Matt had gone she realised that it was as if he had brought with him a breath of fresh country air, and he had left it there with her as a gift.

Her mind was clear again, and although the farm was there as an escape hole she could bolt into, she knew she could not spend the rest of her life fleeing from unpleasant situations. Steve Beaumont had frightened her sufficiently to want to make her run back to where she had come from, but this time she would simply have to stay and face whatever the future had in store for her.

Natalie burst into Loren's office the Friday morning of that same week, and her dark eyes were alight with excitement. 'My boy-friend, Larry, is a technician at the Candlelight Theatre, and he gave me two tickets for the opening night of that new play about——'

'I thought your boy-friend's name was Peter,' Loren interrupted her confusedly.

'Peter?' Natalie stared at her blankly for a moment, then she pulled a face and gestured disparagingly with her hands. 'Oh, no, that was ages ago.'

'Oh,' Loren said stupidly.

'Will you come with me?' Natalie returned to the subject which had made her enter Loren's office in such an excited rush.

'When is the opening night?'

'It's tonight,' Natalie frowned. 'Didn't I mention that?'

'No, you didn't,' Loren smiled tolerantly.

'You will come with me, won't you?'

'I think I'd like that very much.'

'There's one small problem, though,' Natalie scowled. 'My car won't budge an inch.'

'What do you mean, your car won't budge an inch?' Loren demanded exasperatedly. 'Honestly, Natalie, during the past six weeks your car has been in the garage for repairs more often than it has been out.'

'I know,' Natalie grimaced. 'But this time it's not at the garage, and I just haven't got the money to have it towed in for repairs.'

Loren tapped her fingers impatiently on the desk. 'How long have you had this car?'

'Eight months.'

'So it's still under guarantee?'

'I think so,' said Natalie, but she did not sound very sure of her facts. 'I haven't really checked.'

'Well, if you ask me, this garage of yours is trying to make money out of you one way or another, and I think it's time I stepped in and took a look at your car for myself,' Loren announced firmly.

'You?' Natalie asked, disbelief widening her eyes.

'I know a little about cars, and I might be able to locate the fault,' Loren played down her knowledge. 'Would tomorrow morning suit you?'

'That would be fine,' Natalie agreed, still looking a little doubtful, but she brightened a moment later. 'About tonight, Loren. If you don't object to giving me a lift home, then I suggest we stop at your place so that you can change, and after that we can go on to mine. I know my mother would be thrilled if you had dinner with us, and then we could go on to the theatre from there.'

Loren smiled. 'I like the sound of that.'

'That's settled, then.'

Natalie went out of the office in much the same manner she had entered it, and Loren simply shook her head helplessly. It felt very much as if she had just dealt with a boisterous child, and Natalie could be totally impossible at times. She could be adult and sensible the one minute, and innocent and childlike the next, but Loren had become very fond of her despite this often confusing transition.

The rest of the day passed swiftly for Loren, and Natalie's mother had dinner waiting for them when they arrived. Natalie talked incessantly throughout the meal, and if Loren had not pointed out that it was getting late, Natalie would not have had time to wash and change out of her office clothes.

They arrived at the Candlelight Theatre five minutes before the curtin was to go up, and when Natalie produced the tickets they were shown to their seats. The theatre was small, almost intimate, and the décor was plush and modern. It could not seat more than a hundred people, Loren was certain of that, and there were not many vacant seats left.

She studied the programme which the usher at the door had thrust into her hand, and she shivered inwardly as she read the title. *The Ghost of Rachel Wells!* What had she let herself in for?

'Loren,' Natalie nudged her sharply, 'look over there.'

'Where?'

'Across the aisle, two rows down,' Natalie whispered, leaning closer to Loren. 'Isn't that Steve Beaumont sitting there next to that attractive blonde?'

Loren glanced in that direction and felt her heart lurch in her breast. 'Yes, it is him.'

Steve Beaumont had turned his head slightly, giving her a clear view of that strong, familiar profile, then he glanced back at the woman beside him. It seemed as if he was saying something to her and, whatever it was, it made her smile up at him in a way that could only be termed as intimate. Loren's chest tightened, momentarily restricting her breathing, and she lowered her gaze hastily to the programme she clutched in her hands. She stared at it fixedly in an attempt to control herself, and the awful tightness in her chest eased slightly.

The lights were dimmed, and the curtain rose on the first act of *The Ghost of Rachel Wells*. Loren tried desperately to concentrate, but the dramatic, often eerie play made no impact on her. She was too aware of Steve Beaumont seated a little distance from her, and her glance was drawn repeatedly in his direction.

'Damn the man!' she thought angrily, dragging her gaze
back to the dimly lit stage, but her interest waned
steadily in the dramatically portrayed events taking
place beyond the footlights.

There was a short break between the first and the
second act, but there was a longer interval before the
the third and final act, and everyone was eager to go
out and stretch their legs. The foyer was crowded with
people, some of whom had come out for a quick smoke,
or a drink in the theatre lounge, but Loren found
herself searching against her will for that familiar face
while listening half-heartedly to Natalie's incessant
chatter about the superbness of the play.

It was Natalie who saw Steve Beaumont first, and she
nudged Loren in the ribs with her elbow. 'There they
are again, and he's looking this way.'

Cigarette in one hand, and the attractive blonde
clinging to his free arm, Steve Beaumont looked directly
into Loren's eyes across the distance separating them.
His features remained expressionless, giving no initial
sign of recognition, and she had a horrible feeling that
he was going to ignore her when he surprised her by
inclining his head briefly in their direction.

'Well, what do you know!' Natalie breathed beside
Loren. 'He actually greeted us!'

Loren's insides felt quiveringly tense, and her jaw was
clenched so tightly that it almost ached. Her eyes felt as
if they had become welded to Steve as they followed
him and his companion into the lounge, and only then
did she turn to Natalie to say stiffly, 'Let's go inside.'

Natalie glanced at her strangely, but she did not
question Loren as they entered the auditorium and
resumed their seats. Loren made a pretence of studying
the programme, but she was fully aware of those two seats
across the aisle which remained empty until mere seconds
before the lights were dimmed for the final act. She wished

she could match Natalie's enthusiasm for the play, but her concentration had droped to zero, and she breathed an inward sigh of relief when the curtain eventually lowered on the final dramatic scene. She rose with everyone else when the actors appeared on stage to acknowledge the applause, but her actions were automatic, and her applause was merely a polite acknowledgement. She could not wait to get out of there. She wanted to go home, and when the curtains came down for the last time, she literally dragged Natalie out of her seat so that they could lose themselves in the crowd moving slowly towards the exit. Steve Beaumont was somewhere behind her, but she dared not turn her head to glance in that direction, and the tension in her did not relax until they were seated in her Stanza and driving away from the Candlelight Theatre.

Loren was up early the Saturday morning and, dressed in old denims with her hair tied back in a ponytail, she arrived at Natalie's home, as promised, to take a look at her problematic car.

They went down into the basement garage and, pulling up the sleeves of her warm sweater to above her elbows, Loren began her slow but thorough check of the engine. Natalie stood there eyeing her dubiously, and when Loren tugged at some of the wires she heard Natalie's audible, nervous gasp.

'Where did you learn about cars?'

'My father taught me,' Loren answered her absently.

'Have you ever worked on a car such as this one before?' Natalie questioned Loren with a noticeable hint of anxiety in her voice as she peered first over Loren's one shoulder, and then the other.

'No, I haven't worked on a car such as this one before, but all vehicles are basically the same even though the layout might be different.'

'Can you see anything?'

Loren had had a bad night, and she felt agitated as she turned protestingly to face Natalie. 'You're making me nervous. Why don't you go upstairs and keep yourself occupied making us some coffee, or something?'

'Yes, ma'am,' Natalie grinned sheepishly, walking towards the lift in the basement, and Loren sighed with relief when she had gone.

Natalie stayed away almost an hour, but that gave Loren enough time to work on the car without having someone peering anxiously over her shoulder, and she was fastening the last bolt when Natalie stepped out of the lift with a mug of coffee in each hand.

'I hope you noticed that I left you in peace for an hour,' Natalie teased. 'Where do you want your coffee?'

'Put it down somewhere, will you?' said Loren without looking up from her task.

'Have you located the problem?' Natalie questioned curiously when Loren finally straightened.

'Yes,' Loren smiled into Natalie's anxious face. 'Get behind the wheel and turn the key in the ignition.'

Natalie did so, and the engine sprang instantly to life, but Natalie's shriek of excitement could be heard above the sound. '*Whoopee*, it works!'

'Switch it off!' Loren shouted back in response when she had satisfied herself that everything was working as it should and, when Natalie had done so, Loren explained the fault to her. 'I've made a slight adjustment to the rotor arm in the distributor, but it's only a temporary adjustment which is sufficient to get you to the garage on Monday, and I suggest you ask to speak to the manager this time. This car has been fitted with a faulty distributor, and my guess is that it's a factory fault. They have worked on it, I can see that, but if you leave it much longer your guarantee will expire, and you'll end up paying for a new distributor instead of having it replaced free of charge.'

'What does a distributor do, for heaven's sake?'

'It does exactly what its name implies,' Loren smiled tolerantly. 'It distributes the current to the individual sparking plugs in the engine.'

'Which it hasn't been doing, I suppose.'

'Precisely,' Loren nodded, wiping her hands on a grease-stained cloth. 'Other than that there's a hairline crack in the cap of the distributor which caused an internal sparking, and that seized up your car's ignition. I've sealed the crack temporarily, and replaced a few wires, but I strongly suggest you have the distributor replaced.'

Natalie eyed Loren curiously. 'I would never have believed that someone as feminine as you could do such a masculine job!'

'When you've lived on a farm most of your life you learn to do all sorts of things,' Loren laughed as she lowered the bonnet and snapped it shut.

Natalie glanced at Loren with some concern. 'Your hands are covered in grease.'

'I'll clean them under that tap over there,' Loren reassured her, and, armed with a bottle of soapy liquid and a nailbrush, she walked across to the tap which the residents used when they washed their cars.

She scrubbed her arms and her hands, taking particular care with her nails, then she rinsed them off under the tap and dried herself on the towel which she always carted around in the boot of her car.

'I would never have said the chief of Beaumont Engineering liked the theatre,' Natalie changed the subject so swiftly that Loren barely had time to control her features. 'And what did you think of that dishy blonde he had with him last night?'

'She was beautiful,' Loren replied casually, swallowing down a mouthful of coffee.

'I'll say she was!' Natalie grinned wickedly. 'Do you think she's his mistress?'

That distasteful query had been milling through Loren's own mind most of the night, and her voice was unnecessarily sharp when she answered Natalie. 'Mr Beaumont's private life is no concern of ours.'

'Were you jealous?' Natalie probed teasingly.

'Don't be silly!' Loren snapped irritably, but her denial sounded extraordinarily hollow, and her heart skipped a frightened beat which she had no intention of analysing.

'Mother said to tell you you're welcome to stay to lunch,' Natalie announced when they had finished their coffee.

The thought of going back to an empty flat had not appealed to Loren, and she laughed with relief. 'Your mother will have to send me an account one of these days for all the meals I've had with you!'

'She loves having you, and so do I,' Natalie said simply, and Loren knew she had meant it.

Loren had become fond of Natalie's mother over the past weeks, and Mrs Miller had showered her with an abundance of warmth and friendliness. Her homely, sometimes motherly manner had helped to ease Loren's longing for her own parents, and she would always be grateful to Natalie and her mother for that.

Loren did not return to her own flat until late that afternoon, and she soaked herself in a scented bath before changing into clean slacks and a sweater. Natalie's mother had prepared such an enormous lunch for them that Loren was not hungry that evening. She made herself a cup of coffee, and settled down to an evening in front of the television set, but tiredness made her eyelids droop, and she switched off the set when the eight o'clock news came on.

The doorbell chimed loudly before she could put out the lights and go to bed. If she had not been so tired she might have guessed the identity of her unexpected visitor, but she was totally unsuspecting when she opened the door as far as the safety chain would allow and found herself staring up into those mocking, incredibly blue eyes. Her heart thumped against her ribs, and her legs promptly turned into jelly as she heard herself murmur incredulously, 'Mr Beaumont!'

'Undo the safety chain and let me in,' he ordered and, fingers fumbling in nervous haste, she did as she was told.

What was he doing here? What did he want? she wondered as she gathered her scattered wits about her and led the way into the lounge. 'Could I make you a cup of coffee?'

The mockery in his eyes deepened. 'If you promise not to spill it in my lap.'

'I suppose I shall never quite live that down,' she groaned, escaping into the kitchen before he could see the flush of embarrassment surging up into her cheeks.

Her hands were shaking when she switched on the kettle. She set out two cups in a tray, and her heart was beating so uncomfortably fast that she had difficulty in breathing properly. It was quite ridiculous that one particular man's presence could affect her in this way, and she was annoyed with herself for her inability to do anything about it. Steve Beaumont was capable of sparking off something within her which no one else had succeeded in doing before, and it frightened her so much that she dared not risk analysing her feelings. She had no idea what she might discover, but she shied away from whatever it was like a frightened horse shied away from an adder lurking in the veld.

The coffee was ready much too soon, and Steve lay

sprawled out on the sofa when she entered the lounge.
She placed the tray a little hesitantly on the low table,
but he sat up at once, and this time she handed him his
cup of coffee without so much as spilling a drop in the
saucer.

'Black with no milk and sugar?'

'You have a good memory,' he smiled faintly.

'How was your trip to Namibia?' she asked as she
added milk and sugar to her own coffee and seated
herself in the chair facing him.

'Hectic,' he said abruptly, and she noticed for the
first time the lines of strain etched deeply about his eyes
and along the sides of his mouth.

He looked tired, she thought, a compassionate
warmth surging through her, but she checked that
spontaneous feeling almost at once. It would be safer
not to feel any kind of emotion where Steve Beaumont
was concerned, and she resolutely shut her mind to his
masculine appeal while they drank their coffee in
silence.

'Why are you here, Mr Beaumont?' she asked
eventually, hating herself for the tremor in her hand
when she placed her empty cup in the tray.

'I would prefer you to call me Steve.'

Loren chose to ignore his statement. 'You haven't
answered my question. Why did you come here this
evening?'

'I came here because, much as I hate to admit it, our
last meeting was as much a disaster as all the others,' he
smiled twistedly, and she lowered her gaze hastily to
avoid the mockery in his eyes.

'What makes you think this meeting won't end
similarly in a disaster?'

'I'm an eternal optimist.'

Nothing had changed, Loren realised this, and his
goal was still the same, although his approach to it

varied slightly. She felt nervous and agitated, and the sudden inability to sit still made her leap to her feet. 'Mr Beaumont, I can't——'

His fingers snaked about her wrist, stopping her in mid-sentence, and, caught off her guard, she let him pull her down on to the sofa beside him. 'Before you make any rash statements let me say what I've had on my mind all week. I know I was a bit hasty the other evening, but one thing led to another, and I ended up saying things in the heat of the moment which no man ought to say to a woman after their first date.'

Loren was aware of his hard thigh against her own, and she was certain he could feel her pulse racing beneath his fingers. 'If that's an apology, then I accept it, but——'

'Let's try again,' he interrupted her. 'And this time we'll take it a little slower.'

'With the same purpose in mind?' she was forced to ask and, raising her eyes valiantly to his, saw him smile derisively.

'I'm a man, Loren, not a saint, and you're a very lovely woman.'

'You were in the company of a beautiful woman last night,' she reminded him scathingly. 'Why not concentrate on her?'

'There are too many men concentrating on her at the moment.'

'I can't give you want you want,' she protested, knowing that bluntness was the only thing a man like Steve might understand and, wrenching her wrist free of his grasp, she got to her feet to avoid the disturbing contact of his body. 'I have certain principles by which I've always lived, and I don't intend to relinquish them for your sake, or anyone else's.'

'That sounds like a virgin's swan song,' he smiled twistedly as he pushed himself on to his feet and

towered over her. 'I'm saving myself for the right man,'
he mimicked her derisively.

'You have no right to mock me!' she stormed at
him, her tawny eyes sparkling with fury. 'I don't
condemn you for the way you live your life, so don't
condemn, or mock me for the way I choose to live
mine.'

'Dammit, Loren!' he growled harshly, his hands
gripping her shoulders and his eyes burning almost
feverishly down into hers. 'Every time we come near
each other something happens; every time we touch a
spark is ignited between us—and don't tell me you
haven't felt it, because then you're a rotten liar!'

It was true! She felt it now, and she had felt it before.
It was a near-electrifying current that surged through
her, but she knew she had to fight it with every ounce of
strength she possessed.

Her lips parted in protest, but Steve's mouth
swooped down to stifle the words, and her will-power
was severely taxed not to respond to the fire of
his sensually demanding kiss. She only discovered
how successful she had been when he held her away
from him moments later to gaze quizzically into her
eyes.

'Loren?'

'You're wasting your time, Mr Beaumont,' she said
in a surprisingly cool voice as she extricated herself
from his arms. 'No amount of persuasion will make me
change from what I am to what you want me to be—
and besides that, we barely know each other.'

'The latter can be remedied.'

'I have no desire to get to know you better,' she
assured him, and anger darkened his eyes where
mockery had glittered moments before.

'I take that as an insult.'

'Take it as you wish,' she told him, her control

coming close to snapping. 'I'd be grateful if you would
go away now and leave me alone.'

His mouth tightened, and she thought for a moment
he was going to refuse, then that devilish gleam
sparkled in his eyes once again. 'I'll go, Loren, but let
me warn you, I don't give up easily.'

CHAPTER SIX

THE Monday morning started wrong for Loren. She awoke with a dull headache, and when she arrived at the office her electric typewriter jammed for some mysterious and infuriating reason. The technician was still busy repairing it when she was told that Steve Beaumont wanted to see her. Harvey Griffin could give her no explanation for this request, and Loren was nervous and apprehensive when she took the lift up to the fourth floor. A summons to the inner sanctum, as everyone called Steve Beaumont's office, was totally out of the ordinary for anyone other than the directors and heads of departments, and Loren felt a coldness settling at the pit of her stomach.

Mrs Markham looked up from her work when Loren walked into her orderly office, and she seemed to bristle with displeasure.

'One moment, please,' said Mrs Markham, obviously expecting Loren, and, lifting the receiver of the telephone on her desk, she pressed the required button. 'Miss Fraser is here to see you, Mr Beaumont,' she spoke into the mouthpiece, then she replaced the receiver on its cradle and directed her gaze at Loren. 'You may go in.'

Loren stared at the panelled door, and swallowed nervously, but her step was light and firm on the carpeted floor as she approached it. The brass handle was cool beneath her fingers when she opened the door, and her heart thudded uncomfortably somewhere in the region of her throat when she stepped into the spacious, airy room.

A padded leather sofa and matching chairs stood at one end of the room, and they were arranged around a low circular table, but Loren's glance shifted uneasily towards the opposite end of the room where Steve Beaumont stood behind the enormous ebony desk. He was staring out of the window with his broad, formidable back turned towards her, and his hair was once again a burnished copper in the early morning sunlight that streamed into the office.

'Come in and close the door, Miss Fraser,' he addressed her with an authoritative formality which intensified that coldness at the pit of her stomach, then, without turning to face her, he added: 'You'll find a notebook and pencil on the desk, so I suggest you make yourself comfortable.'

Loren closed the door as he had instructed, and approached the desk. There was a slight tremor in her hands when she picked up the notebook and pencil, and she sat down quickly on the padded, upright chair when it felt as if her legs wanted to give way beneath her.

She studied his tall frame with a puzzled expression in her tawny eyes. 'Do you expect me to take dictation, Mr Beaumont?'

'Any objections?' he demanded harshly, turning for the first time to look at her.

'No, I——' She faltered, disconcerted by the impact of his cool blue gaze as it met hers. 'None at all.'

'Take down the following,' he said abruptly, and when she had flipped open the notebook on her knee, he rattled off several paragraphs of highly technical data which might have frightened the life out of someone with less experience, but Loren's pencil flew over the paper. Her nervousness forgotten, she took down every word despite the incredible speed at which he was dictating. If he was attempting to fault her, then he was in for a surprise, she thought with a mixture of anger and amusement. His deep-throated voice halted abruptly after five minutes of non-stop dictation, and when Loren glanced up enquiringly, he asked: 'Did you get all that?'

'Yes, Mr Beaumont,' she replied, still totally bewildered by the reason for this exercise.

'Read it back to me,' he ordered, turning his back on her once again to stare out of the window, and she obediently waded through the pages filled with pencil squiggles. The technical terms made no sense to her, but she read each word exactly as he had dictated it, and when she came to the end of it she looked up to find him studying her intently. A flicker of something close to admiration lit his eyes, but it was gone so swiftly that she might have imagined it.

'May I know what this exercise was in aid of?' she broke the awkward silence between them.

He seated himself in the wing-backed swivel chair behind his desk and took his time lighting a cigarette before he explained. 'My secretary, Mrs Markham, has to go into hospital for an operation, and she'll be away for six weeks as from next Monday. I shall expect to see you in her office tomorrow morning at eight-thirty so that she can acquaint you with the routine.'

Loren felt her back stiffen. 'But I——'

'That will be all, Miss Fraser,' he announced coldly, cutting into her protest and dismissing her simultaneously.

She could argue with him elsewhere, but not here where he was the kingpin, she realised helplessly. She rose to her feet to return the notebook and pencil to the desk where she had found it, then she walked out of his office without a backward glance, and closed the door quietly but firmly behind her.

'I gather you're going to take my place while I'm

away?' Mrs Markham asked, halting Loren in her angry stride.

'So I've been told,' Loren replied, turning to look into those grey eyes surveying her doubtfully, and a faintly cynical smile curved her mouth. 'Don't look so troubled, Mrs Markham. I'm not normally as clumsy and incompetent as you appear to think I am.'

The older woman's eyebrows rose sharply above her clearly dubious eyes. 'I sincerely hope you prove me wrong!'

Loren did not linger to prolong the conversation, and walked out of the office to take the lift down to the Accounts department. The light of battle was in her eyes, and she entered Harvey Griffin's office just as he was putting down the telephone.

'Mr Griffin, I have——'

He gestured her to silence. 'I've just spoken to Mr Beaumont, and he's explained the new arrangement to me.'

'But I don't——'

'I suggest you ask Natalie Miller to come to your office,' Harvey Griffin cut short her protestations. 'She's relieved here before, but I daresay she might need to have her memory refreshed about certain things.'

Loren closed her eyes momentarily, telling herself to remain calm, then she looked down into Harvey Griffin's bespectacled eyes and said what she had been trying to say from the moment she had walked into his office. 'Mr Griffin, I don't want to go up there to Mr Beaumont's office.'

'I'm afraid you'll have to, Miss Fraser,' he brushed aside her statement almost impatiently. 'It's all arranged.'

'Surely there must be someone else who could take Mrs Markham's place while she's away?'

'Mr Beaumont has specifically asked for you,' he stated flatly.

'And what Mr Beaumont wants, he usually gets,' she murmured, labouring heavily under her defeat.

'I beg your pardon?'

'Nothing,' Loren sighed exasperatedly. 'I was merely thinking out loud.'

She went into her own office and sat down behind her desk, but it took a few moments to calm herself sufficiently before she called Natalie on the telephone and asked her to come down to her office.

'Why so glum?' Natalie asked curiously when she entered Loren's office moments later.

'You're taking over here as from tomorrow, so you'd better let me start refreshing your memory in case we have to go over something again this afternoon,' Loren explained briskly.

'Why am I taking over your job?' Natalie asked with a mixture of anxiety and surprise in her dark eyes. 'Where are you going?'

'Mrs Markham is going into hospital for an operation, and I shall be taking her place as she'll doubtless need time to recuperate.'

Natalie pursed her lips and whistled softly, her eyes wide beneath her raised brows. 'How long will she be away?'

'Six weeks, I'm told.'

'I don't envy you at all having to take over from that tyrant of a woman, and I know I'm going to miss you down here,' said Natalie after a thoughtful pause.

A lump rose in Loren's throat which was partly as a result of the frustration boiling up inside her, but she was determined not to give in to it. 'Don't get sentimental, Natalie, or I might burst into tears!'

The rest of that day was spent re-acquainting Natalie with the details of Harvey Griffin's office routine, and when Loren went home that evening she knew only too well that the following day it would be her turn to listen and take note. Mrs Markham was a meticulous woman, everyone knew that, and Loren found herself viewing the next few days with a great deal of trepidation. Her thoughts inevitably turned to Steve Beaumont. He had been coldly distant that morning, treating her like a subordinate stranger, but it would be easier to work for him in such circumstances. A nasty suspicion arose from the recesses of her mind that he had an ulterior motive for installing her as a replacement for Mrs Markham, but she thrust it from her mind at once.

Under Mrs Markham's eagle-eyed supervision, Loren spent the remainder of that week acquainting herself with the mammoth task of acting as the managing director's secretary, and Mrs Markham did not believe in half measures. She was going to be away for six weeks, and she was obviously determined that everything should continue in much the same way as if she would actually be there. Loren was no stranger to the rigours of office routine, and she learned quickly, making notes where necessary, and asking questions when she was in doubt.

Steve Beaumont maintained his polite but aloof manner towards her, and Loren's nerves swiftly settled down to normality. She could cope with him, and with herself under these conditions, and she prayed silently that he would continue to keep his distance during the coming weeks.

'Whatever you do, Miss Fraser, don't fumble,' Mrs Markham warned on the Friday afternoon when it was almost time to go home. 'Mr Beaumont is a very busy man, and he can't afford the time wasted on mistakes.'

'I'll do my best, Mrs Markham,' Loren promised, hiding her amusement behind a solemn expression.

And do make sure that he has lunch sent up to him

on those days when there's no necessity for him to go
out to a business luncheon.'

There was genuine concern in her brisk voice, and
Loren glanced at the older woman speculatively. 'You
really care about him, don't you, Mrs Markham?'

'He works very hard, and he often neglects himself,'
Mrs Markham revealed, looking faintly embarrassed.
'I've never known anyone to drive themselves as fiercely
as Mr Beaumont, and he's not doing so merely for
himself, but also for the welfare of his staff.'

Loren did not comment on this information, but it
had allowed her a brief insight into the character of the
man who headed this vast company. She realised for the
first time the tremendous responsibility attached to his
position, and she could imagine the stress and strain
which must so often accompany it. It made her see him
in a totally different light, and what she saw awakened
her compassion and respect.

'There is one other thing,' Mrs Markham interrupted
Loren's thoughts. 'Mr Beaumont quite often has very
bad attacks of migraine, and he seldom carries the
prescribed tablets with him, but I keep a supply handy
here in my desk drawer.'

'Is there something else I ought to know?' Loren
asked when Mrs Markham's expression was fraught
with indecision.

'Yes,' Mrs Markham confirmed, looking vaguely
embarrassed once again. 'Women are quite often
inclined to pester Mr Beaumont, so do please confirm
with him whether he wishes to speak to them before
you put them through to him.'

Loren hid her amusement yet again behind a grave
exterior. 'I'll do that.'

'Thank you,' Mrs Markham sighed. 'I think that's
all.'

Loren watched her cross the room to stare out of the

window, and it was as if she sensed a certain loneliness beneath that cloak of brisk efficiency which the older woman always donned.

'Mrs Markham?' Loren touched her arm lightly to bring her out of her thoughtful stance. 'I hope the operation is a success, and I shall keep you posted while you're convalescing.'

'Would you?' Mrs Markham asked, visibly surprised, and Loren nodded gravely.

'I'll come and see you in hospital as soon as you're allowed visitors.'

Mrs Markham's sharp features relaxed into one of her rare smiles. 'That's very kind of you, Miss Fraser.'

When Loren went home that afternoon the realisation hit her for the first time that she would be returning to that office on the Monday morning without Mrs Markham being there to draw on for information. She would be on her own with Steve Beaumont, and it did not help much to shut her mind to the knowledge that, with each meeting, her feelings for him grew more unmanageable. She dared not give way to the fears which stormed through her mind; if she did then she might be tempted to take flight, and that would be cowardly.

Loren spent the weekend tidying up the flat and seeing to her clothes. It was not an activity she had planned, but she knew she had to do something to keep herself occupied or she would go crazy thinking about the weeks ahead of her. Natalie arrived on the Sunday evening, full of bounce, and bubbling with excitement. Her car had at last been returned to her in tip-top condition, and the reason for her excitement was a long, informative letter from her sister in which she had related some of their experiences on their tour.

Loren welcomed the diversion from her own thoughts, but the conversation inevitably turned to the subject she would have preferred to avoid when Natalie asked: 'How do you feel about tomorrow?'

'Nervous,' she confessed with a grimace.

'I bet the old dragon primed you about all the chief's likes and dislikes,' Natalie laughed.

'Mrs Markham is not an old dragon,' Loren defended the woman she had come to know during the past week. 'She's a very nice lady, actually, and I think also a lonely one.'

'I suppose you're right, only . . .' Natalie smiled impishly and shrugged characteristically, 'she does seem like an old dragon sometimes.'

Loren could not dispute that statement; she had thought the same on a number of occasions during the past weeks, but she now knew differently after working so closely with Mrs Markham. She was a woman who took pride in her work, and like most efficient private secretaries, she concerned herself with lightening the load of her employer's responsibilities.

The shrill ring of the telephone sliced through Loren's thoughts, and she rose quickly to answer it.

'Miss Fraser?' Steve Beaumont's voice addressed her formally when she had lifted the receiver to her ear, and her pulse rate accelerated to quite an alarming pace.

'Yes, Mr Beaumont,' she replied in a controlled voice, and saw Natalie's eyes widen when she glanced in the mirror above the telephone table.

'I won't be coming into the office until after lunch tomorrow,' he informed her in that distant voice she was beginning to hate. 'Cancel all my appointments for the morning, or postpone them if you can.'

'What about the directors' meeting which is scheduled for ten-thirty?'

'Damn!' his voice exploded over the line, jarring her nerves. 'Postpone the meeting until Tuesday morning at

the same time, and notify everyone of the change, but
there's one other matter which is quite urgent. 'You'll
find the Dormehl contract on my desk, and I want it
typed and ready for signing tomorrow afternoon.'

'Certainly, Mr Beaumont.'

He said an abrupt 'Goodnight', and the line went
dead, severing the almost hostile link between them, but
Loren felt vaguely annoyed when she dropped the
receiver on to its cradle.

'What was that about?' Natalie wanted to know
when Loren had resumed her seat.

'Mr Beaumont won't be in until after lunch
tomorrow, and there's something he wants me to do for
him,' Loren explained briefly.

'You're getting the best deal out of Mrs Markham's
sojourn in hospital,' Natalie complained humorously.
'I'm saddled with old Griffin, but you get to be at the
beck and call of a man as handsome as Steve
Beaumont!'

Loren's lovely mouth curved downwards at the
corners in a faintly cynical smile. 'Want to swop?'

'I would if I could,' Natalie laughed mischievously,
'but the trouble is the chief has set his sights on you,
and there's no way he'll look at me.'

'Oh, lord, don't say things like that!' Loren moaned,
alarm spreading through her like a bush fire fanned by
the wind.

'What are you afraid of?'

'I have a nasty feeling that if I knew what I was
afraid of I'd resign tomorrow and go back to Aberdeen
post-haste,' Loren confessed gravely, but Natalie found
it highly amusing, and her laughter followed Loren into
the kitchen when she went to make them some coffee.

Knowing that Steve would not be at the office on
Monday morning made Loren less nervous about going

to work, and the first thing she did when she arrived at the office was to cancel the ten-thirty meeting and inform everyone that it had been postponed until the Tuesday morning. The Dormehl file was on Steve's desk, as he had said, and she worked on it after cancelling the rest of his appointments for the morning.

The hours passed swiftly and Loren was much too busy to think of anything other than her work. She dealt speedily and efficiently with all the incoming calls, and she had the contract typed and waiting on Steve's desk when he walked into the office at two o'clock that afternoon.

'I want you to send the biggest bouquet of fresh flowers you can get to Mrs Markham. She's in ward 3A of the General Hospital,' he said, pausing beside her desk and flipping open the private telephone index next to the telephone. 'That's the name and telephone number of the florist I usually patronise, and have the account sent to me at this address.'

'Any message?' Loren asked as he walked away.

'No message is necessary, simply say it comes from me,' he said, and the next moment the panelled door of his office was closed firmly behind him, but somehow his presence still seemed to linger in the room with her.

Loren telephoned the florist and placed the order, charging it to Steve's account as he had instructed. She worked on steadily until their tea was brought in, and when she took his tray through to him, he looked up from the papers he had been studying.

'Have your tea here with me and bring me up to date with what happened this morning,' he instructed, and she poured his tea as she knew he liked it before she went through to her own office.

She was back a few seconds later with a cup of tea in one hand and a notebook and pencil in the other, and when she seated herself to face him across the wide expanse of his desk she found she had to steel herself against his disconcerting blue gaze.

She waded systematically through the notes she had made, pausing occasionally to give him time to bring his own appointment book up to date and to jot down a few names of people he would have to contact, but there was one item which she left until last.

'A Miss Priscilla Ramsay telephoned this morning,' Loren informed him, an odd tightness inside her when she called to memory that lilting femine voice on the telephone. 'She said you know her number, and would you please call her back.'

His expression did not alter except for a slight narrowing of his eyes when they met hers. 'Was there anything else?'

'That was all, Mr Beaumont.'

She consulted her notebook, and checked swiftly once again through the notes she had made, but she felt his eyes on her, and when she looked up, he pushed his empty cup towards her. 'You can pour me another cup of tea, and pour one for yourself if you wish.'

'I shan't have more tea, thank you, Mr Beaumont,' she declined politely, getting up to pour his tea before she returned to her own office.

'Miss Fraser,' he halted her before she reached the door. 'Priscilla Ramsay is the lady who accompanied me to the Candlelight Theatre. Please remember that I'm not available should she call again.'

The mental picture was complete, that lilting voice now had an attractive face attached to it, and that tightness in her chest eased a fraction as she turned to face him. 'What if she accuses me of not passing on her message?'

'I'm sure you're inventive enough to think up something suitable,' he said, a sardonic smile curving his sensual mouth briefly, and Loren went out of his office wondering what, exactly, he had meant by that.

Contrary to what she had feared, Miss Priscilla Ramsay with the lilting voice did not call again to question Steve's neglect in reacting to her message, but had she done so that afternoon, Loren would have had a legitimate excuse to pass on to her, for Jim MacDonald was the first of a steady stream of people to come in and see Steve, and he was kept busy until it was time to go home.

Loren did not visit Mrs Markham in hospital until the Wednesday evening, and when she walked into the semi-private ward she found Steve's secretary lying against the pillows with her eyes closed. She looked so pale that Loren was actually afraid for a moment as she approached the bed quietly. It was most unusual to see this normally brisk and efficient woman lying there so pale and lifeless, and Loren felt a warm tide of compassion rising within her as she went forward to touch the hand resting on the white sheet.

'Mrs Markham?'

Her eyelashes flickered, and her grey eyes mirrored her physical discomfort, but there was also surprise in their depths when her eyes met Loren's. 'I never thought you'd really come and see me here in hospital.'

'But I said I would, didn't I?'

'I know you did,' Mrs Markham smiled tiredly, 'but people often say things they don't really mean.'

Loren pulled a chair closer to the high bed, and sat down. 'How are you, Mrs Markham?'

'I feel as though I've been put through a crusher, but I'm told the third day is usually the worst, so I imagine I'll feel much better tomorrow,' the older woman grimaced slightly.

Loren's glance shifted to the large bouquet of white chrysanthemums and golden carnations which stood on the locker beside the bed. 'Are these the flowers Mr Beaumont sent?'

'Yes, aren't they lovely?' Mrs Markham smiled, and her sharp features softened miraculously. 'Did you know Mr Beaumont came here to the hospital early Monday morning before I was taken into the theatre, and that he remained here until after I came round from the anaesthetic?'

'I didn't know,' Loren replied, discovering yet another revealing side to Steve's character which he kept so well hidden beneath that often harsh, dynamic exterior. 'I thought he was out somewhere on business.'

'He's a wonderful man, you know,' Mrs Markham told her with some gravity. 'He has his faults, like most of us, and at times he can be totally ruthless, but he can also be kind and generous, and on the administrative side I've always found him extremely fair.'

If Mrs Markham had been thirty years younger then Loren might have classifed her statement as 'hero-worship', but from a woman of almost fifty Loren could only accept it as a revealing truth from someone who had a clear insight into the character of the man she worked for and admired.

Loren did not comment on the older woman's remark, there was no necessity to do so, and she changed the subject by discussing what had occurred in the office during the past three days. Mrs Markham listened with interest, and she gave advice where necessary. Loren appreciated this, but she did not want to tire Mrs Markham, and she left after half an hour with the promise to come again the following evening.

Loren settled down into her new office routine without difficulty, and, after her daily visits to the hospital, she began to see Steve in a totally different light. Working in such close proximity with him she also made a few discoveries of her own, but not all of them were new to her. He was a brilliant man, respected by his male colleagues for his clever, intellectual brain, and highly sought after by the women for his physical attributes. As Mrs Markham had warned, women very often pestered him, and his annoyance had clearly indicated that he was a man who very much preferred to do his own hunting instead of having his prey fall readily at his feet.

It was towards the end of her second week as Steve's secretary that she discovered the outwardly impregnable man could be vulnerable as well. She walked into his office shortly before the lunch hour to find him sitting on the sofa with his head buried in his hands, and his face distorted with pain.

'Are you ill, Mr Beaumont?' she asked anxiously.

'Migraine,' he explained with a twisted smile as he looked up at her with eyes that seemed not to focus properly. 'I get it now and then.'

'Have you taken anything for it?'

'Can't find my confounded tablets,' he grunted, the sheen of perspiration on his furrowed brow, and his jaw jutting out as he clenched his teeth.

'I'll get you some,' Loren said quickly, remembering the tablets in her desk drawer, and she was back in his office moments later with a glass of water in one hand and a small phial of tablets in the other to find him sitting once again with his head in his hands. 'Mr Beaumont?'

He raised his dark head slowly to take the glass from her, and held his other hand palm upwards for her to shake two of the prescribed tablets into it. He swallowed them down, and Loren's heart contracted with sympathy when she saw the knotted muscles in his neck. This man was in agony, that much was obvious, and she had the ability to help him.

'Thanks,' he murmured, slumping back against the backrest of the sofa as she took the glass from him and placed it beside the phial of tablets on the low, circular table.

'Loosen your tie, and undo the top buttons of your shirt,' she ordered, making a swift decision, and he obeyed without questioning her while she walked round to the back of the sofa to stand behind him.

She had never before touched him of her own volition, and her heart thumped oddly in her breast, but she did not waste time doubting her decision. His skin was warm and slightly damp beneath her fingers as she expertly massaged the knotted muscles, inducing them to relax while the tablets did the rest. She saw his wide shoulders sag beneath the white shirt and slowly, very slowly, the muscles in his neck regained their elasticity beneath the kneading, rhythmic motion of her massaging fingers.

'Hm ... that feels good,' he sighed eventually, his head falling back against her, and she looked down on his now unlined forehead where the thin film of perspiration was the only indication of the agony he had suffered moments earlier. 'You have magic in your hands.'

His eyes were closed, his lashes extraordinarily thick, and when she ceased the impromptu massage she raised her hand automatically to brush a thick strand of hair away from his forehead. It felt surprisingly soft beneath her fingers, almost silky, and she experienced the most incredible desire to touch the thick, neatly trimmed mahogany hair with her lips. Startled by the intensity of her feelings, she backed away from him sharply.

'Lie down and relax while I order lunch to be sent up to you,' she said, walking away from him, and her voice sounded stilted in her effort to control the tremor in it.

'Loren?' he stopped her when she reached the door, and she turned warily to see him stretching his long, muscular length out on the sofa as she had suggested. "Ham sandwiches and coffee will do, and order something for yourself to be brought up here.'

Loren nodded, but his eyes were already closed, and she went into her office to telephone through to the canteen. She felt shaky, and quite unlike herself. Her fingers still tingled with the feel of him, and she did not risk returning to the office behind the panelled door until the tray of sandwiches and coffee had been brought into her office.

'Feeling better?' she asked when she entered Steve's office ten minutes later to find him still in a reclining position on the sofa.

'Much better, thanks to you,' he smiled faintly as he swung his legs to the floor and sat up. 'What have you got there?'

'Ham sandwiches and coffee for both of us,' she said, placing the tray on the low table and pouring their coffee.

Steve remained where he was on the sofa and Loren seated herself in the comfortably padded chair close to it. Neither of them spoke while they ate their sandwiches, but it was not an uncomfortable silence, and it was only when he leaned back against the sofa with his second cup of coffee in his hands that Steve spoke for the first time.

'Were you very angry with me for making you come up here as a replacement for Mrs Markham?'

She was startled by his query, but she answered him with her usual honesty. 'Yes, I was angry.'

'You suspected that I had an ulterior motive?' he shrewdly interpreted her thoughts at that time, and she did not bother to deny it.

'Yes, I did suspect something like that,' she smiled, not attempting to avoid his piercing, faintly mocking glance.

'You were right.'

Her smile froze as his bald statement sent little shock waves along her still taut nerves, and renewed anger put the chill of ice into her voice. 'After a confession like that do you honestly expect me to continue working for you?'

'You've visited Mrs Markham in hospital every evening since last Wednesday,' he surprised her with his knowledge, but she failed to see the connection until he added smoothly, 'You will stay on out of loyalty to her, if not to me.'

His accuracy in judging her character made her realise that he had been studying her as much as she had been studying him, and it sent a curious sensation rippling through her.

'At times you actually frighten me,' she confessed as she watched him light a cigarette and exhale the smoke through his nostrils.

'I believe I've behaved impeccably these past two weeks.'

'You have,' she admitted gravely, and a gleam of sardonic amusement entered his eyes.

'What is there to be afraid of, then?'

What *was* there to be afraid of? she asked herself. Steve was a man prone to pain and joy just like any other, but still she remained wary of him. She sensed the danger like an animal which stood quivering in the bush when the scent of the hunter drifted towards it on the breeze, but unlike the animal she had nowhere to run to, and no place to hide.

'I'll clear away these things and have them collected,' she evaded his query nervously.

'What's the rush?' he drawled lazily, his disturbing gaze following her movements as she returned the plates and the cups to the tray.

'You have a Mr Fenwick coming to see you at two, and it's almost that now,' she told him, glancing at her wrist watch, and he rose swiftly to his feet.

'I'd forgotten,' he frowned, and she did not stay to see him straighten his tie and put on his jacket.

Loren carried the tray through her office, and called the canteen to collect it before Mr Fenwick arrived. They had a busy afternoon ahead of them, but Loren found herself wondering how she was going to concentrate after the disturbing conversation she had just had with Steve Beaumont. To become too deeply involved with him would be like riding the wind, and she would come crashing down to earth when she least expected it. She could never bear the uncertainty of such a relationship, and she would have to guard against it.

CHAPTER SEVEN

THE atmosphere in the office altered considerably during the next few weeks. Under pressure of work Loren began to lower her guard, and in the process she discovered the finer qualities of the man who had initially frightened her into believing that no woman was safe with him. At times her mind warned that Steve's impeccable behaviour was merely a front, and that he had simply altered his form of approach, but it was a warning she found herself ignoring.

Mrs Markham had been released from hospital two weeks after her operation. She looked fit and well whenever Loren visited her at her flat during weekends, but the doctor had insisted that she stay away from work for the full six weeks, as he had stipulated before her admittance to hospital.

'It's most annoying,' she complained one Saturday afternoon when Loren paid her a visit. 'There's really nothing wrong with me, and I'm perfectly capable of resuming my duties at the office.'

'I think your doctor is the best judge where your health is concerned,' Loren said wisely. 'Take this opportunity to have a complete rest, and you have my word that when you return to the office everything will be the same as when you left it.'

'I no longer doubt that,' Mrs Markham smiled. 'Mr Beaumont has been giving me excellent reports on his frequent visits.'

Loren was startled by this disclosure, but she did not comment on it, even though it remained with her for some time to come. Steve could be arrogant and egotistical at times, but he was obviously not bigoted when it came to showing concern for the woman who had done so much for him in the office over the past years.

Steve flew to Namibia two weeks before Mrs Markham was due to return to the office. The purpose of this trip was to finalise the details of a project his company would be in charge of, and for some inexplicable reason Loren had felt uneasy about it from the moment he had asked her to make the flight arrangements. It was with the greatest difficulty that she had prevented herself from asking him not to go. He would have despised her if she had voiced her fears, and she had finally shut her mind to that nagging little voice in her subconscious. Steve left for Windhoek on the Monday afternoon flight without Loren saying a word, and she could only pray that he would arrive back safely on the ten-thirty flight Thursday morning.

Loren buried herself in her work to help pass the time, but that feeling of dread persisted. She was being ridiculous, she told herself repeatedly, but on the Thursday morning she was as restless as a ewe about to give birth. She could not explain it even to herself, but it was as if she was mentally holding her breath while waiting for something dreadful to happen. Jim MacDonald would be in the vicinity of Jan Smuts airport about the time Steve's flight was due to arrive from Windhoek, and it was arranged that he would meet Steve and bring him back to the office. Loren's glance darted all too frequently towards the electric clock on the wall that morning, and at noon she was almost ready to sigh with relief.

The shrill ring of the telephone on her desk made her nerves jar violently, but she calmed herself sufficiently to answer it.

'Miss Fraser?' Jim MacDonald's abrupt voice barked in her ear. 'I'm calling from Jan Smuts airport, and I want to you to cancel all Steve's appointments for this afternoon.'

Fear caught at her throat, but she eased away the tightness with trembling fingers. 'Has his flight been delayed?'

'There's been an accident,' his reply sent a chill of terror racing into her veins. 'The plane Steve was on crashed at take-off from Windhoek airport.'

The blood drained from her face to leave her deathly white. 'Oh, my God, is he——'

'I don't know yet,' Jim MacDonald cut into her petrified query. 'No information has come through about the passengers, and I strongly suggest you keep this to yourself until I've received further news. There's no sense in getting everyone in a panic until we know all the facts.'

'Will you call me as soon as you hear something?' she heard herself asking in a voice which sounded much too calm to belong to her.

'I'll do that,' he confirmed, and the line went dead with equal abruptness.

Loren fumbled the receiver back on to its cradle, and she fought desperately against the swirling mist which was threatening to envelop her. She had never fainted in her life before, and she was not going to do so now. She had to stay calm and rational no matter what the circumstances. Steve would expect it of her. There had to be no tears, and no hysteria. It was something she knew he could not tolerate.

Steve! His name echoed like a wailing siren through her tortured mind, and fear, like the talons of an eagle, tore at her heart and pierced her soul. She loved him, she knew it now, and the painful knowledge came as no surprise to her. During the past two weeks she had unintentionally opened her heart and her mind to him. She had allowed him to walk in and become the most vital part of her existence and, if he died, a part of her would die too.

'Oh, God!' she groaned, burying her white face in her trembling hands. 'Please don't let him be dead! I couldn't bear it if he died!'

Tears caught at her throat and stung behind her closed eyelids, but she dared not give in to them. She took a deep, steadying breath, and lowered her hands to stare fixedly at the telephone. There were quite a number of calls to make, and she had to keep herself busy somehow. She flipped open her diary and systematically went through the list, telephoning everyone to cancel their appointment with Steve for that afternoon. One client could not be contacted, and she had to leave a message for him to give her a ring as soon as he was available.

With that task taken care of, she could not settle down to doing anything else while she waited for Jim MacDonald to telephone the latest news through to her. She paced the floor restlessly; it was the only thing that made the chill of anxiety bearable for her as the minutes dragged endlessly, and that was how Natalie found her an hour later when she walked into the office.

'Aren't you coming to lunch?' she wanted to know, pausing beside the desk to observe the unaccustomed sight of Loren walking back and forth across the carpeted floor.

'I'm having something sent up here,' Loren lied, the thought of food at that moment nauseating her.

Natalie shrugged and turned to leave, but something must have made her turn back to study Loren more closely. 'You look as if you've seen a ghost, if you don't mind my saying so.'

'I'm a little tired, that's all, and I . . . Just a moment!'

Loren cut her explanation short when the telephone started ringing shrilly, and she literally leapt at it to snatch the receiver off the hook. 'Mr Beaumont's office.'

'Le Roux here,' said an unfamiliar male voice. 'I believe you've been trying to contact me.'

'Yes, Mr Le Roux.' Loren only barely managed to conceal her disappointment. 'I'm afraid something unexpected has come up, and we'll have to cancel your appointment with Mr Beaumont for this afternoon.'

'Could I see him tomorrow, then?'

'Oh, God, I hope so,' Loren prayed silently, but aloud she said: 'I'll make a provisional appointment for three-thirty tomorrow afternoon, if that will suit you?'

'That would suit me fine,' he replied, and Loren replaced the receiver moments later to find Natalie eyeing her curiously.

'Has the chief been delayed in Windhoek?'

'Yes, he——' Loren bit her lip and sat down heavily behind the desk. Her head felt as if it wanted to burst, and fear was gnawing away at her insides like a horde of termites let loose in a timber mill. 'God, Natalie, I'm not supposed to tell anyone, but I can't sit here a moment longer with these terrible thoughts pounding through my mind.'

'What's wrong?' Natalie asked, seating herself on the corner of the desk close to Loren and, when their eyes met, the truth spilled from Loren's lips.

'The plane Steve was on crashed moments after taking off from Windhoek airport.'

Natalie's face paled and her eyes widened in horror. 'He's all right, though, isn't he?'

'We don't know, and that's the worst part of it,' Loren groaned, dangerously close to tears, but she controlled herself with an effort. 'Jim MacDonald is at the airport waiting for news about the passengers, and he'll let me know as soon as he's heard something.'

Confiding in Natalie lightened Loren's burden slightly, and she did not protest when Natalie ordered sandwiches and tea to be brought to her office.

'My mother always says that in an emergency one ought to keep one's strength up,' Natalie announced firmly. 'Knowing you, I'd say you came to work without having breakfast, and if you don't eat something now you're in danger of collapsing.'

Loren did not argue with her, and when the sandwiches and tea arrived she actually found herself eating what Natalie had piled on to her plate, but she might just as well have been eating paper for all she cared.

The internal telephone rang, but it was Natalie who snatched it up. She listened for a moment, then said icily, 'No comment, and you'd better keep your mouth shut if you know what's good for you.'

'What was that about?' Loren queried, but she had already guessed the answer.

'The news has leaked, I'm afraid,' Natalie confirmed her suspicions. 'One of the chaps in the drawing office heard about the disaster on his car radio, and my guess is he's already told quite a few people before plucking up enough courage to phone direct to this office.

'Oh, dear,' Loren murmured concernedly. 'A panic among the staff was exactly what Mr MacDonald had wanted to avoid.'

'There's no way this information could be kept from them once the news media have made it public knowledge, and there's bound to be a bit of a panic at the moment.'

Panic! Loren could relate to that word. She had never felt so panicky and afraid in her entire life, and that icy dread which had settled in her chest made her shiver from time to time.

The second hand of the electric clock on the wall seemed to be moving with deliberate slowness as the agony of waiting piled the tension higher. It was almost two o'clock, and Loren felt ready to snap like a spring which had been coiled too tightly.

The shrill, piercing ring of the external telephone sliced through the silence, jarring her nerves, but this time she reached it before Natalie.

'Information has just come through,' Jim MacDonald's grim voice reached her amid the noise of heightened activity at the airport. 'Eleven dead and thirty-six injured. No names have been given, but the uninjured passengers are on a special flight to Jan Smuts, and they should arrive within the next half hour.' He paused to swear softly. 'This place is a madhouse of newshounds from the press, but I'll call you when I have something more definite.'

The line went dead abruptly and left Loren clinging to that ever thinning thread of hope. She had to go on hoping, it was her only form of survival at that moment, and without it she would simply fall to pieces.

'What's the news?' Natalie intruded on her frantic thoughts.

'Eleven dead and thirty-six injured,' Loren repeated Jim MacDonald's message parrot-fashion. 'The uninjured passengers are on a special flight to Jan Smuts.'

Natalie's hand gripped Loren's shoulder. 'You're really cut up about this, aren't you?'

'Natalie, if he's dead, I——' She bit back the rest of her revealing statement, and made a last desperate attempt to steady herself before she glanced up at the clock. 'You'd better get back to your office, and don't answer any questions if you're approached for information.'

She did not put up an argument, but said simply, 'Let me know when you hear something.'

Loren nodded without speaking, then she was alone with her fears, and the terrifying knowledge that it would be foolish of her not to prepare herself for the worst. Jim MacDonald could give her no guarantee that Steve would be on that Boeing winging its way to Johannesburg, and she would simply have to go on waiting like everyone else.

She got up to resume her pacing, restless to the point where she could scream. Her ears were waiting for the jarring sound of the telephone, but her eyes were on the clock, and her heart was beating away each agonising second as if it had become wired to that electrical device against the wall.

'How much longer?' she asked herself in anguish. 'How much longer do I have to wait?'

More than half an hour had elapsed before the call came through which she had been expecting. She felt herself break out in a cold sweat as she snatched up the receiver, and her insides felt like a solid block of ice.

'Miss Fraser?' Jim MacDonald's voice seemed to bellow into her ear. 'Steve is alive, and we ought to be at the office in about another half hour.'

Her relief was so intense that she could not speak for a moment, but Jim MacDonald did not wait to hear her reaction, and the dialling tone was purring in her ear before she whispered brokenly, 'Thank God!'

Loren was shaking so much that she could barely replace the receiver, and for a few brief moments she allowed herself the luxury of shedding a few forbidden tears. She had kept them locked within her during these agonising hours since Jim MacDonald's first call, but her rigid control had snapped a little, and it was at this point that Natalie chose to walk into her office.

'I was worried about you,' she explained with concern. 'I made some excuse to old Griffin, and came up quickly to find out if you've heard anything.'

'He's alive, Natalie,' she smiled shakily, dashing away her tears as she eased her weight off her trembling legs and sat down behind her typewriter.

'Thank God for that!' Natalie sighed with obvious relief. 'When do you expect him?'

'Jim Macdonald said a half hour.'

'I'd better get back to my own office,' Natalie smiled, glancing at the clock. 'I'll see you this evening.'

Loren leaned back in her chair and closed her eyes for a moment while she fought to regain her composure, then she touched up her make-up to hide the evidence of the tears she had shed. Steve was alive. *Alive!* And God knew she had never been more thankful about anything else in her life. He was alive, and that was all that mattered.

Half an hour felt like an eternity before she heard Steve's deep-throated voice down the passage, and it was followed by Jim MacDonald's booming reply. Loren leapt to her feet, torn between rushing out to welcome Steve back, or remaining where she was. 'Stay calm, and don't make it too obvious,' she warned herself, and with that thought in mind she sat down again behind her desk.

Steve and Jim MacDonald's conversation ceased abruptly, and her heart was hammering wildly when she realised that only one set of footsteps was approaching her office. She swallowed convulsively, squared her shoulders, and the next moment she was looking into those deep blue eyes which she had feared she might never see again. Speechless with emotion, and unable to tear her eyes away from him, she found herself taking in every detail of his beloved appearance. His face was grim and pale beneath his tan, and his eyes were haunted and watchful. His suit was not of the quality he usually wore, for the jacket seemed to fit too tightly across the width of his shoulders and when she glanced at the unbuttoned shirt collar she doubted if it could ever be fastened about his strong throat.

'The clothes were very kindly lent to me after mine were ruined in the accident,' he explained as if he had read her thoughts, but Loren was too choked to comment on this, and he added in a clipped voice, 'Come through to my office, and bring your notebook and pencil with you.'

She stared at him in bewilderment as he strode past her desk and pushed open the panelled door into his office, and only then did she come alive. She snatched up her notebook and pencil and followed him into his office, to find him standing in front of the oak cabinet pouring himself a stiff whisky. He swallowed it down quickly to pour himself another, and only then did he sit down behind his desk.

He was surely not going to sit down there calmly and work as if nothing had happened? she asked herself in blank amazement as she seated herself gingerly on the edge of her chair. He had lived through a terrible experience, and he ought to relax and unwind, but instead he took off the jacket which was a size too small, and opened his briefcase.

'With my appointments cancelled for this afternoon we might as well work our way through this mountain of information I have here,' he announced, and Loren's jaw almost dropped to indicate her shocked surprise.

With a wad of papers in front of him he started dictating, rapidly and without hesitation, and Loren found herself racing to catch up after her initial lack of reacting instantly.

Work was actually the antidote she had needed after the traumatic hours she had spent wondering whether he was alive or dead, and, as the project unfolded on paper before her, she realised that this was what Steve had needed as well. Idleness, after what they had both

lived through in their separate ways, would have been
the worst possible thing. She had been ready to crack
when he walked into the office and, she presumed, so
had he, but instead she felt some of the tension and the
strain easing out of her until she could almost say she
was relaxed.

They worked on steadily until four-thirty that
afternoon, with Steve pausing only occasionally to
swallow down a mouthful of whisky, or to light a
cigarette, and when at last he leaned back in his chair,
she met his glance and decided that she loved him more
in that moment than ever before.

'I think that's all for today,' he said, crushing his
cigarette into the ashtray and, taking that as a
dismissal, Loren rose to her feet, but she could not go
without letting him know to some extent how she felt.

'Steve . . .' He looked up when she faltered, and she
swallowed nervously when their eyes met. 'I'm so glad
you're back safely.'

She saw his hands clench on the desk, and a terrible
bleakness entered his eyes. 'So am I.'

She did not wait to prolong the conversation, she was
too perilously close to tears, and she hastily escaped
into her own office where she had to make a desperate
attempt once more to calm herself.

When Loren went home at five that afternoon she
had not quite succeeded in shaking off the tension
which held her insides knotted firmly in place. Her own
rigid control was partly to blame for it, and when she
arrived at the flat she bathed and changed into
comfortable beige slacks and a green woollen sweater.
She left her hair loose, and brushed it until it shone like
gold, but she had not yet relaxed when the early evening
news was flashed on to the television screen. She could
hear the newsreader's voice from the bedroom,
monotonously recording the events of the day, and it

seemed to intensify that tightness in her chest to the extent that she walked into the lounge with the intention of switching off the set. Her hand reached out for the button, but at that precise moment the charred wreckage of a Boeing was flashed on to the screen.

Loren stood frozen, listening against her will to the detailed account of the accident in which Steve had been involved. The Boeing had developed technical difficulties an instant after take-off, the nose had dipped and the plane had hit the tarmac with a hundred and seventy-five passengers and crew members on board. The horror of it all was on the small screen in front of her as they showed flashes of the aftermath of the accident with fire-fighting teams attempting to put out the blaze. At Jan Smuts airport the television cameras had awaited the arrival of some of the passengers from Windhoek, and the next moment Steve's ruggedly handsome face came into focus. Someone questioned him about the accident, but he refused to comment on it, and shouldered his way out of sight. The other passengers were, however, eager to talk, and Loren found herself listening intently to what one elderly woman had to say.

'Mr Beaumont risked his own life when he climbed back into the burning wreckage to help two injured passengers who'd been trapped in their seats,' she said. 'He'd barely carried the last man out to safety when the Boeing became an inferno in which no one would have survived. It was terrible!'

Loren could not bear to listen to more of it, and she switched off the television to find that she was shaking as if she had a raging fever. She lowered herself into a chair, attempting to control the tremors that shook through her, but she was totally incapable of doing anything about it. She was shaking like a leaf, and dry sobs were tearing along her throat. Finally the tears came; hot, stinging tears chased each other down her cheeks until she put her head down on her arms and wept uncontrollably.

It was a long time before she managed to control herself sufficiently, and she had to admit to herself, albeit reluctantly, that it had done her the world of good to cry. She felt considerably better, and no longer so tense, but when she rinsed her face in cold water and stared at herself in the bathroom mirror, she realised that the stormy tears she had shed had created havoc with her face. Her eyes were red and puffy, and so was her nose. She would have to do her make-up all over again, and this time she took a great deal more care with it than before.

Natalie arrived at the flat shortly after seven that evening, but the only trace of Loren's recent tears was a faint redness about her shadowed eyes, and an unusual paleness in her cheeks which she had not succeeded in hiding. The anguish she had suffered that day was still too fresh in her memory, and cold shivers raced up and down her spine every time she thought of how close Steve had come to death.

'Did the chief say anything to you?' was the first thing Natalie asked as Loren led the way into the lounge.

'We never discussed the incident.'

'I saw him on the early T.V. news.'

'So did I,' Loren shuddered, convinced that the frightening sight of that burning wreckage would remain for ever in her mind. 'I'll make us some coffee.'

Natalie followed her into the kitchen, and, although they changed the subject, their conversation was subdued as if the disastrous incident that day had flung its sombre cloak on Natalie as well.

An odd silence settled between them when they drank their coffee in the lounge, and Loren decided to probe

this unusual reticence between them when she looked
up to see Natalie observing her with a strange look on
her face.

'Is something wrong?' she asked.

Natalie shook her head, but her face retained its
solemn expression. 'You're in love with him, aren't
you?'

It was an irrefutable statement from someone who
had shared Loren's anxiety, and to deny her feelings
would be futile. 'Am I that transparent?'

'To me you are,' Natalie replied gravely, 'but I doubt
very much if anyone else would have noticed.'

Loren was silent for a moment, then she laughed
mirthlessly, but her laughter ended in a groan that
reflected the misery she felt. 'Oh, Natalie, you're
looking at the biggest fool this side of the Equator!
There's no future in loving a man like Steve, and
heaven knows I didn't want to love him.'

Natalie wisely did not comment on this, and they sat
there in silence for a moment until the doorbell pealed
loudly throughout the flat. They stared at each other, a
query in their eyes, then Loren got up and crossed the
room to unlatch the door.

Steve seemed to fill the doorway with the height and
breadth of him, and her heart leapt into her throat with
a force that made her catch her breath. In brown
corded pants and matching jacket he looked so vitally
alive, and so devastatingly masculine, that she was
made to realise once again how tragic it would have been
if his life had ended in that horrifying disaster.

'May I come in?' he interrupted her silent appraisal,
and she coloured slightly when she realised that she had
been staring.

'Yes, of course,' she said hastily, opening the door
wider to let him in, and when he passed her she could smell
the pleasing odour of his familiar masculine cologne.

'Good evening, Mr Beaumont,' Natalie greeted him politely, jumping a little nervously to her feet, and he acknowledged her with a brief nod, but his eyes sought Loren's while Natalie glanced uncomfortably from one to the other. 'Look, I was going anyway. I'll see you tomorrow, Loren.'

'I'll come to the door with you,' Loren offered, wrenching her eyes from Steve's, but Natalie gestured her to remain where she was.

'I know my way out.'

Steve's compelling glance captured Loren's before Natalie had closed the door properly behind her, and during the ensuing silence she was conscious only of the heavy thudding of her heart, until Steve spoke.

'I hope you don't mind my coming here this evening, but I could think of nowhere else to go to escape being pestered by the press at my home.'

He looked like a little boy lost at that moment, and she had to fight down the impulsive desire to place her hands on his clean-shaven cheeks and to kiss him on the lips.

'Would you like a cup of coffee?' she asked, dragging her eyes from his, and wishing her heart would not beat quite so fast.

'Yes, thanks,' he sighed, lowering himself into a chair and stretching out his long legs while Loren escaped into the kitchen.

She was considerably calmer when she returned to the lounge a few minutes later with his coffee, and while he drank it she found herself observing him closely. There was still that hint of paleness about his mouth, and his eyes had a haunted look that made her heart ache for him. The grooves running from his nose to his mouth seemed deeper, more pronounced, and the hand that held the cup had a faint tremor in it which was quite unlike Steve.

'You look tired,' she observed quietly when she had removed the empty cup from his hand and had placed it on the tray.

'I am tired,' he confessed surprisingly, then his face went strangely ashen as he sat forward in his chair and buried his face in his hands. 'God, Loren, it was terrible! Women and children screaming, and big men blubbering like babies.'

She had never thought she would live to see him like this, and her love and compassion for him rose like a tide within her to bring her down her knees in front of him. Her hand gently touched his bowed head, and she marvelled once again at the softness of his hair as she slid her fingers in a tender caress down to the nape of his neck.

'Steve . . .' she began softly, but he looked up then, and the words of comfort seemed to lock in her throat when their eyes met.

The nightmare of it all was like a cloak about them, shutting them off from the rest of the world, and Loren had never felt as close to anyone before. It was as if their minds had locked to become one, and she knew his anguish as if it were her own.

'It isn't a pleasant thing looking death in the face,' he said hoarsely, giving her a glimpse of the naked fear he must have felt at the time of the accident, and then, somehow, they were in each other's arms.

He held her tightly, drawing her up between his knees, and her arms wound themselves about his neck of their own volition. She wanted to comfort him; she wanted to shield him from the awful memory of what had happened, and when he shuddered against her she instinctively pressed her body closer to his. Her throat felt choked, and a stinging moisture was building up behind her closed eyelids which she did not have enough time to blink away before he held her a little away from him.

'Tears?' he questioned her in surprise, catching a drop of moisture on his finger before it rolled too far down her cheek.

'I'm sorry,' she apologised, swallowing convulsively. 'It's simply reaction after all the hours of wondering whether you were alive or dead.'

'Would it have mattered one way or the other?' he asked softly, his hands framing her face so that she had no option but to meet his eyes, and what she saw there robbed her of the desire for anything other than the truth.

'It would have mattered very much.'

She heard him catch his breath above the thundering of her heart, and then he was kissing her, her eyes, her lips, her cheeks, her throat, and then her lips once more. They were light little kisses, devoid of passion, but they aroused a need within her which she could not quite understand herself at that moment.

His arms tightened about her, and he lifted her on to his lap to cradle her against him like a child. For long endless seconds she found herself looking up into his eyes, and the intensity of his gaze quickened her pulse until at last his mouth came down to claim hers. It was different this time. He kissed her with a hunger that parted her lips, and he drew a matching response from her that seemed to light a fire deep down inside of her. The only prominent thought in her mind at that moment was that she loved him, and that she had so very nearly lost him. It made her arms tighten almost convulsively about his neck to deepen their kiss, and she made no attempt to stop him when his hand slid beneath her sweater to caress the smooth skin at her waist. His touch aroused the most pleasant sensations, and although she knew she ought to stop him, she remained perfectly still when she felt him unhook the catch of her bra.

Loren had never allowed a man such intimacies before, but with Steve it was different, and she felt neither embarrassed nor ashamed by it. It felt so perfectly right when his hand cupped her breast, and the probing caress of his fingers sent little shivers of pleasure rippling through her. She ought to stop him, but she also wanted him to go on touching her and, with these conflicting emotions to cope with, she left it too long. Drugged by his fiery kisses, she lay supine in his arms when he carried her into the bedroom, and her lips were eager once again for the sensual warmth of his mouth when he lowered her on to the bed.

CHAPTER EIGHT

LOREN's lips moved beneath Steve's with the intensity of
her feelings as he kissed her with a lingering passion,
and she felt too dazed with love for him to protest when
he drew back slightly to ease her sweater off over her
head. He flung it aside, and her lacy bra followed the
same path. His eyes, aflame with unmistakable desire,
burned down into hers as he shrugged himself out of his
jacket and unbuttoned his shirt. The nakedness of his
wide, muscled chest inflamed her senses and, when he
leaned over her to gather her into his arms, the
abrasiveness of his chest hair against her breasts
awakened a strange new excitement within her.

'Loren ... my beautiful Loren,' he murmured
throatily, trailing hot kisses along the sensitive column
of her throat down to her breasts.

Her lips were parted, and she was breathing jerkily as
his tongue and his lips caressed her breasts until the
rosy peaks hardened with a desire which was almost a
pain. Her mind, dulled though it was, recognised his
expertise as a lover, and her body responded to his
sensual, arousing touch until she was inflamed with an
aching need that made her hips arch involuntarily
towards his.

'Loren, Loren ...' he murmured her name thickly
against the soft, rounded cushion of her breasts, and
her fingers became locked in his mahogany hair as a
moan of ecstatic pleasure burst from her lips.

Loren could not recall afterwards at what stage he
had undone the button at the waistband of her slacks,
and neither could she recall when he had pulled down

the zip, but she was rejoicing in the muscled smoothness of his shoulders beneath her frantically caressing hands when she felt his fingers dipping beneath the elastic of her skimpy underwear.

'Steve!' she croaked in a voice which was unfamiliar to her ears as she came to her senses with a jolt, and she hastily stayed the action of his hand as it strayed towards the most intimate part of her body. 'Oh, Steve, *no!*'

'Let me love you?' he pleaded hoarsely against her mouth even though he had halted his caress. 'Let me stay with you tonight and love you?'

Her body was on fire with an aching need for a fulfilment she had never known, and she was tempted almost beyond reason, but her mind flashed out a desperate warning which she was forced to heed. For her it would be a union of love, but for Steve it would simply be yet another conquest, and she could not have her love for him degraded by indulging in an affair which she knew would lead nowhere.

'No, Steve, I—I can't,' she heard herself denying them the one thing they both wanted so desperately at that moment. 'I can't let you stay, and I don't want you to make love to me.'

'Loren,' he groaned, seeking her mouth, but she evaded his lips, and somehow managed to free herself of his arms to roll away from him.

She snatched up her sweater and held it up against her as she sat up. She was embarrassed suddenly by her nakedness and when he tried to tug it away, a desperate cry broke from her lips. 'No! I beg of you, don't!'

He sat up slowly, clearly confused by her sudden refusal, and his eyes were dark with a mixture of desire and understandable anger. 'If you don't want me to make love to you, then why the hell did you let it go this far?'

Loren was asking herself that same biting question. 'We were both emotionally overwrought after what had happened today,' she tried to explain away what had occurred between them. 'I didn't mean to let it go this far, but relief sometimes plays nasty tricks on people after they have suffered a tremendous anxiety, and I wouldn't want us to do anything which we might regret in the morning.'

'I want you, Loren, and I can't see myself regretting anything if you let me stay,' he said persuasively, trailing sensual fingers across her bare shoulder and down the hollow of her spine.

She jerked away from the devastation of his touch and jumped to her feet while still clutching her sweater to the upper half of her body. 'You may not regret it, Steve, but I know I would.'

He stared at her long and hard, his eyes raking her from head to foot in a way that made her feel vaguely uneasy, then he got up and pulled on his shirt. He pushed the ends into his pants without bothering to fasten it, and shrugged himself into his jacket. He was angry, she knew that, and she also knew that he had every right to feel that way, but she could not let him go without trying to salvage something out of this unhappy and awkward situation.

'Steve . . .' she pleaded, her throat tight with tears of remorse, 'please try to understand.'

'Go to hell, Loren Fraser!' he snarled at her so savagely that she actually backed a pace away from him. 'You're nothing but a tease, and that, in my opinion, is the lowest any woman can get!'

'Steve!' she gasped, white and trembling, but he stormed out of the bedroom without a backward glance, and moments later the outer door was slammed so viciously that she flinched where she stood riveted to the carpet in the bedroom.

She felt stunned, as if he had slapped her physically. *A tease,* he had called her, and in his opinion the lowest any woman could get. Was that what she was? Is that truly how he saw her? A tease, a temptress who led men on only to drop them at the crucial moment? Her hands tightened on the sweater she still clutched against her body, and a shiver of self-disgust rippled through her when she realised that *that* was exactly how she had behaved. She had led him on; stupidly and ignorantly she had encouraged him, only to shy away when she had realised that they were coming too close to the physical act of love. *Love!* That was the key word. She loved him, but for Steve it would have meant no more than yet another scalp to add to his belt, and the next day she would have been classified as one of his many victories, while to her it would have been the total giving of her mind, her body, and her soul.

Loren groaned as she fell across the bed and buried her hot face in the pillow where his head had lain moments ago. She wished she could cry, but no tears came to relieve her of the aching misery that tore through her. She could still feel the touch of his hands on her body, but there was no joy in the memory, only a burning humiliation at the thought of what she had allowed.

Loren had had no idea how she was going to face Steve the following morning, but somehow they slipped into their familiar routine as if nothing unusual had happened the previous day. Steve was extraordinarily busy that day, and so was Loren. The telephone went mad with people wanting to discuss the air disaster with him and, on instructions from Steve, she had to deal with them as best she could.

They left the office a little later than usual that afternoon, and went down in the lift together. She wanted to talk to him, to explain if she could, but somehow the words had become locked in her throat. How could she explain without making him aware of her true feelings? She glanced covertly at the stern-faced man beside her, and her cheeks went hot at the memory of the intimacies they had shared the previous evening. Looking at him now it was difficult to believe him capable of the emotions he had displayed, but when she thought of her own ecstatic response she was even more astounded.

Their footsteps echoed hollowly in the now empty parking garages, and when she reached her car she thought he was going to walk on without speaking to her, but he stopped beside her and touched her shoulder briefly.

'I owe you an apology, Loren,' he said when she raised questioning eyes to his, and her breath caught in her throat with a mixture of embarrassment and relief.

'No, I'm the one who should apologise,' she corrected hastily, and the rest of her words came out in an impulsive, unrehearsed rush. 'What you said last night was true. I *did* lead you on. God knows I didn't mean to, but that doesn't alter the fact that I did. I should have called a halt sooner, but I somehow got carried away, and what happened afterwards was entirely my own fault.'

Half way through that guilt-ridden speech she found she could no longer sustain his glance, and she lowered her eyes to the polished leather of his expensive shoes. Her voice drifted off into silence, and she felt oddly worse than when she had started.

'Your generosity makes me feel ashamed of myself, and that's something I haven't felt in a long time,' he remarked somewhat drily, but, when he placed a finger beneath her chin to tilt her face up to his, she found his expression grave instead of mocking. 'I can't let you condemn yourself in that way, Loren, when the truth is that I went to you last night with the intention of making love to you. I wanted to shut out the memory of what had happened, and I wanted to forget it all in your arms.' He smiled sardonically when her tawny eyes widened. 'Does that shock you?'

'No,' she replied, lowering her gaze when he released her chin. 'I can understand how you felt.'

'And you can forgive me?'

'Yes,' she whispered in absolute sincerity, but the voice of a hateful demon at the back of her mind whispered those painful words, *He needed a woman last night, and you would have been as good as any other.*

'You're not only beautiful, Loren, you're quite unique,' Steve's voice intruded on her painful thoughts. 'You're calm in a crisis, and totally efficient. You're gentle and understanding, and generous in the giving of yourself to others. You will be generous in the giving of your body too, and some day some lucky man is going to succeed where I failed last night.'

He walked away from her and left her with the feeling that she had been hit in the stomach. She got into her car and drove herself home, but his last words seemed to reverberate through her mind. *Some day some lucky man is going to succeed where I failed last night.*

Some day some lucky man! Oh, God, there would be no other man! There was only *one* man, and if she could not have him, then she wanted no one else. *No one!*

Loren went to see Mrs Markham on the Saturday afternoon, and the conversation, needless to say, revolved around Steve and the terrible incident which had occurred at the Windhoek airport, but somehow Loren found herself discussing the long hours of anxiety quite calmly. Mrs Markham had fortunately not known that Steve had been on that flight, and it was only when she watched the television news on Thursday evening that she had discovered his involvement. She had been shocked, but not as greatly disturbed as those who had known and feared for his life.

'I can't wait to get back to the office,' Mrs Markham announced when Loren was about to leave. 'I've worked nearly all my life, and I don't think I could bear to sit at home for much longer than another two weeks.'

Loren smiled, but she did not comment on that remark. Two weeks, she thought when she went down in the lift to where she had parked her car. She had two weeks left as Steve's secretary, and after that ...! She did not want to think about it just yet, but she had partly made up her mind about what she was going to do.

The first two days of the following week were more than simply hectic at the office. Something had gone wrong with the Namibia project, that much Loren had gathered, for Jim MacDonald spent more time in Steve's office than in his own, and his booming voice nearly overpowered Steve's harsh, distinctly authoritative voice during the lengthy discussions which could almost be termed as arguments if one did not know that these two men had too much respect for each other to indulge in a verbal brawl. They drank gallons of coffee and smoked cigarettes until a blue haze hovered in the room which nearly choked Loren each time she entered it to find them poring over the papers scattered across Steve's desk.

'I want to leave on the early morning flight to Windhoek tomorrow, and I'd like to return again on the late afternoon flight on Friday,' Steve told Loren on the Wednesday morning, and her insides coiled into a knot of fear at the memory of his last flight to Windhoek, but she forced herself to remain silent. 'Will you make the necessary arrangements?'

'Would you like me to arrange the usual accommodation?'

'No accommodation will be necessary,' he announced grimly. 'As you may have gathered, we're having problems with one of our installations, and I'll most probably be working through the night.'

'I'll see to it at once.'

'And, Loren——?' he stopped her before she reached the interleading door. 'Do you think you could meet me at the airport on Friday evening?'

'Certainly,' she replied without hesitation, walking out of his office and closing the door firmly behind her.

Jim MacDonald came in half an hour later, and Loren did not have the opportunity to speak to Steve again until a few minutes after five that afternoon, when she walked into his office to find him standing in front of his desk. He was frowning down at the papers he held in one hand, and in the other he held a glass of whisky in which the ice tinkled as he swivelled it absently.

'It's all arranged,' she told him, consulting her notebook. 'Your flight leaves at seven tomorrow morning. 'There's a stop-over at Upington, which means that you'll only get to Windhoek after ten. Your return flight on Friday leaves Windhoek at six-fifteen in the evening and arrives at Jan Smuts at nine. Your ticket will be waiting for you at the airport tomorrow morning.'

'Thank you,' he said abruptly, flinging the papers on to his desk and draining his glass of whisky.

'I've also telephoned the Windhoek office and arranged for a car to be waiting for you when you arrive.'

'You're an angel, Loren,' he smiled down at her suddenly in that bone-melting way, and her pulse was none too steady when she turned from him, but his heavy hand on her shoulder halted her hasty retreat into her office. 'I want you to know that I appreciate what you've done for me these past weeks,' he said, thrusting home the fact that she had two days left to act as his secretary before Mrs Markham returned to her post.

'I did only what was expected of me,' she protested, avoiding his eyes, and intensely aware of his hand resting on her shoulder.

'You did more than that,' he insisted. 'You kept the office running efficiently in Mrs Markham's absence, and I know that's not how it would have been if I'd enlisted the aid of someone else to stand in for Mrs Markham.'

'Thanks for the compliment,' she smiled, adopting a faintly teasing air as she carefully eased herself away from him to escape his touch. 'Perhaps one day you'll give me a good reference.'

'I'll give you a dreadful reference so that no one will take you on, and in that way I can be sure you'll stay here.' His voice was stern, and so was his expression when she glanced at him quickly, but there was a hint of laughter in his narrowed eyes which slowly disappeared during the ensuing silence as they faced each other. The atmosphere was suddenly charged as if with electricity, Loren felt it in every tingling nerve, but he turned away from her and lit a cigarette. 'I'll be working late tonight, so I suggest you go home.'

Loren stared at his broad back, and the muscles moving beneath his silk shirt. His hair grew strongly into his neck, and she stifled the longing to touch it as she murmured a cool 'Goodnight' and walked out of his office.

Loren spent two quiet days at the office without Steve.

She had a mountain of typing to get through, and she accomplished it despite the numerous incoming calls which she had to deal with. She made notes for Steve, and she left a few for Mrs Markham to keep her up to date, but she worked at an easy pace to keep herself occupied in order not to think about Steve, who once again had to board a Boeing at Windhoek. The memory of his last return flight must still be as fresh in his memory as it was in hers, and remembered fear still sent icicles charging through her veins whenever she thought of what could so easily have happened.

'Why so gloomy?' Natalie wanted to know some time after Loren had joined her in the canteen for lunch on the Friday, and Loren smiled wryly as she studied the girl, who had kept up a bubbling monologue from the moment they had sat down to eat.

'You're so chirpy that anyone else would appear gloomy to you,' Loren accused lightly.

'If I'm chirpy then it's because I can hand old Griffin back to you on Monday,' Natalie grinned impishly. 'Now you can tell me why you're so gloomy.'

Natalie's grin was infectious, and Loren smiled back at her. 'I'm gloomy for the same reason.'

'I don't blame you,' Natalie laughed so loudly that severeal heads swung in their direction, but she was unconcerned and took her time sobering. 'The chief's away again, isn't he?' she asked eventually.

'Yes,' Loren replied with forced casualness, pushing aside the plate of food she had barely touched, and pouring their tea. 'He'll be back this evening,' she confided, but she did not add that she would be meeting him at the airport.

'Do you know what I overheard Jim MacDonald telling the chief the other day?' asked Natalie, scraping her plate clean with her fork. 'He told the chief that he was getting soft in the head, and that he'd been making too many errors lately to continue securing a healthy future for the company.'

'He's overtired and he needs a holiday,' Loren defended Steve.

'That's what Jim MacDonald advised. "Take a long holiday," he said,' Natalie quoted him, making an attempt to mimic his booming voice. 'And come back more like the man you used to be.'

'I wonder if he'll take Mr MacDonald's advice,' Loren sighed, recalling how she herself had seen the strain and tension of Steve's responsibilities become etched in deep lines about his mouth and eyes.

'The chief didn't sound too keen on the idea, I must tell you,' Natalie replied, and Loren would not have been surprised if she had been told that Steve had strongly opposed the idea.

Loren returned to her office at two, and somehow the afternoon sped by much too swiftly. She was, in a way, not looking forward to meeting Steve that evening, but she did not stop to think about it as she cleared away her personal things and left the office intact for Mrs Markham's return on Monday morning.

The guard at the security gate no longer carried out an inspection of her car. He knew her by sight, as he did most of the other employees and, after lifting the boom, he saluted smartly when she drove through. The traffic was heavy at that time of the day, but, after almost three months in Johannesburg, Loren had discovered that there was no sense in taking secondary roads in the hope of reaching her destination sooner, and she had simply been forced to accept the fact that, at times, she would have to travel home at a snail's pace.

She dressed herself warmly on that cool August night when she arrived at the flat, and forced herself to eat something even though she was not hungry. There was still plenty of time before she would have to leave for the airport, but somehow her stomach felt churned up as if she were racing against the incessant ticking of the clock. She tried to read, but she could not concentrate, and she finally switched on the television to watch a programme which she seldom bothered to watch. It helped, though, to settle her nerves, and she left in good time to reach the airport before nine. She had not taken the busy night life into consideration, and in the end it took her much longer to get to Jan Smuts than she had imagined it would. It was difficult to find parking close to the main building, and when she finally entered the arrival hall the flight from Windhoek had already landed.

Loren searched the faces of the passengers streaming into the building, but it was some minutes before she saw that familiar tall figure standing some distance from her. He had obviously been one of the first to enter the building, and she could see him searching the packed arrival hall with an almost impatient glance.

'Steve!' she cried, elbowing her way towards him, and a faint smile lit up his tired features when she reached his side.

'I thought for a moment you'd forgotten to meet me.'

'I had a little difficulty getting parked,' she explained as they walked swiftly towards the exit, and out to where she had parked her car. 'You'll have to direct me to your home, or would you prefer to drive?' she asked, glancing at him over the Stanza's roof.

'You drive, and I'll direct you,' he said abruptly, flinging his briefcase on to the back seat and easing his long body into the front passenger seat.

Loren did not argue, and when they left the airport grounds, he directed her through the city towards Houghton. This was the first time she would see his home, and she felt strangely nervous about it. She had no idea what to expect, and she caught her breath in surprise and pleasure when she finally drove through the impressive iron gates and up the long drive towards the house. It was a mansion, not a house, she decided, gazing at the carved pillars supporting the balcony above the imposing entrance. The spacious grounds were well lit, giving her a glimpse of something which looked more like a park than a private garden, and she parked her Stanza close to the steps leading up to the entrance.

'Is this where your father used to live?' she asked curiously, turning to face the silent man beside her. 'I mean, has this always been your home?'

'Yes,' he said abruptly, reaching over the seat to get his briefcase. 'Do you like it?'

'It looks very . . .' she paused, searching for the right word, but she settled for, '. . . impressive.'

'Come inside and I'll take you on a conducted tour,' he suggested, and although a part of her wanted to accept, there was a part of her that rejected the idea.

'I don't think so,' she declined politely. 'It's late, and I really must go home.'

'Loren,' he sighed, leaning towards her and placing a persuasive hand over hers on the steering wheel, 'come in and have a drink with me, while I unwind. Please?'

A thousand little nerves seemed to come alive at his touch and, to her dismay, she found she could not refuse him. 'I'll come in for a while, but I shan't be able to stay long.'

'I accept that,' he said abruptly, and she left her car parked where it was to accompany him up the steps towards the ornately carved oak door.

The door was opened before they reached it, and a white-coated Chinese bowed low as they entered, his dark, slanted eyes darting a respectful but disinterested glance at Loren.

'Thank you for taking care of everything for me, Lee,' Steve smiled at him. 'You may go home now.'

Lee bowed low again, murmuring something in his own language, and this time Loren saw the deep scar that ran from his left temple down to his chin. Steve intercepted Loren's faintly horrified glance and, as the Chinese disappeared silently, he placed his hand beneath Loren's elbow to lead her from the spacious hall into the living-room with its odd, but attractive assortment of furniture which had obviously been collected on various travels across the globe.

'I met Lee on a trip to China,' Steve explained, reading the query in her eyes correctly. 'He was in a spot of bother at the time, and afterwards he insisted on coming out here to South Africa to work for me.'

'You saved his life?' Loren asked, seeing in her mind that raised scar on the man's cheek, and making a wild guess at the reason for his attachment to Steve.

'I wouldn't put it quite like that,' Steve smiled twistedly. 'One extra man at his side was enough to send his assailants packing.'

Loren sensed that he was playing down his own part in that incident, but she did not press the matter. 'You brought him out here with you?'

'Yes,' Steve said abruptly. 'I made the necessary arrangements with the Immigration authorities. That was almost fifteen years ago, and in the interim he's found himself a charming wife who's an equally excellent cook when the need arises, and he has two small sons of whom he's very proud.' He flung himself down into a chair and closed his eyes. 'I think we'll leave the conducted tour of the house for some other time. Right now I need a stiff whisky!'

Loren's glance darted about the room and settled on the teak cabinet in the corner. She walked towards it, opened it, and found what she was looking for. She poured a whisky for Steve as she knew he liked it, and she took the liberty of pouring a small glass of wine for herself.

'You really ought to be in bed, Steve,' she told him, the ice tinkling in the glass when she handed it to him.

'I'm much too tense to sleep,' he grunted, his eyes meeting hers, and when he removed his jacket she could see the bunched up muscles beneath his shirt.

'What you need is a massage to relax you completely,' she said impulsively without pausing for thought, and a sensual smile curved his mouth.

'Would you care to oblige?'

Loren lowered her gaze, and embarrassment tinted her cheeks a delicate pink. 'I might.'

'If you go up the stairs and turn right on the landing, then my room is the second door on your left,' Steve enlightened her with a challenging light in his eyes, and a little devil inside her made her accept the challenge.

'I'll give you ten minutes to shower and get into bed.'

He stared at her for a moment as if he was doubting his own ears, then he smiled that twisted, mocking smile, and with his glass of whisky in his hand, rose to his feet and walked out of the living-room.

'I must be going out of my mind,' Loren rebuked herself angrily, but it was too late to do anything about it. She had made the offer, and she would have to follow it through.

She drank her wine slowly, using the stipulated ten minutes to take in her surroundings. Above the fireplace hung a portrait of a man who was undoubtedly Steve's father. They had the same high forehead, the same coppery tint to the otherwise mahogany hair, and the same incredibly blue eyes. The mouth was slightly different, Loren noticed. Steve's mouth was sensual, perfectly chiselled, but his father's was thin, almost cruel, despite the hint of humour in the eyes. It was a handsome face, like Steve's, and she wondered if he, too, had come home some nights looking so unbearably tense and tired.

Loren glanced at her wrist watch. The ten minutes were up. She nervously drained her glass, and placed it on the small rosewood table beside a chair from the Edwardian era. Steve's directions were easy to follow, and she found his room without difficulty.

The door stood slightly ajar, and when she pushed it open she was confronted with the sight of him lying propped up against the pillows with a silk sheet draped across the lower half of his tanned, muscular body. Into the wooden headboard of the giant-sized bed had been carved the figures of a man and a woman locked in a passionate embrace. The colour deepened in her cheeks, and she hastily averted her eyes only to find herself staring somewhat hypnotically at Steve's naked torso with the dark hair on his chest trailing a narrow path down to his navel. She swallowed convulsively, and wondered for a moment what the devil she was doing there in his bedroom, but she steadied herself at once. This was not the first time in her life she was looking at a man's naked chest, she tried to tell herself, but that did not seem to help her very much. She could still recall the roughness of his chest hair against her breasts, and the mere thought of it made her heart beat so hard in her throat that she could hardly breathe.

'Are you coming in?' he mocked her, flexing his taut shoulder muscles. 'Or are you going to stand there staring all evening?'

Motivated into action, she walked towards the bed, and her footsteps were silent on the deep pile of the carpet. She saw the exhaustion etched so deeply on his face, and her emotions eased slowly into deep compassion. He needed her in that moment; he needed her ability to ease the tension out of his taut body as her father so often needed to have the pain massaged

out of his injured back. Think of this man as your
father, she told herself. Impossible! Her nervousness
evaporated, however, and her pulse rate quietened
down to a near normal pace. She had done this often
enough for her father, which meant that she was not a
novice in this field, and she began to feel quite cool in
the face of what she had to do.

CHAPTER NINE

'You haven't finished your whisky,' Loren accused Steve when she saw the ice melting in the drink he had apparently needed so much earlier.

'I thought I'd leave it for a nightcap if I find I can't sleep,' he explained, and she could not decide whether he was being serious or whether he was mocking her, but she did not linger on the query.

'Drink it now,' she ordered briskly. 'When I'm finished with you, you'll feel drowsy enough, and in no need of that kind of inducement.'

In the dimness of the bedside light his sensual smile was devilish. 'That conjures up the most exciting and tantalising thoughts!'

'Shut up!' she snapped, her pulse quickening. 'Drink your whisky, and turn over on to your stomach.'

'Yes, ma'am,' he laughed softly, but he did as he was told. He drank his whisky down in two gulps, and turned over on to his stomach, but in the process the sheet dipped lower to give her a clearer view of his lean hips where his skin was several shades paler than the rest of his body.

'Do you possess a bottle of oil of any description?' she asked, willing her pulse to slow down.

'You'll find a bottle of suntan oil in the bathroom cupboard, and that's all there is, I'm afraid.'

The adjoining bathroom was tiled and mirrored with a sunken, oval-shaped bath, and a shower cubicle behind frosted glass. Steve's clothes had been flung across a chrome and leather bench, and sheer habit made Loren pick up the damp towel he had left lying on the floor. She draped it neatly over the towel rail, and found the oil she needed in the cupboard above the basins which had been built into a tiled slab.

Loren sat down on the bed beside Steve moments later, and she cautiously lifted the sheet a little higher, but her action did not go unnoticed. He laughed softly into the pillow, and she was glad he could not see her burning cheeks.

She concentrated on his back, her glance sliding from the wide shoulders tapering down to slim hips, and she could see the muscles bunched up beneath the smooth, deeply tanned skin. Her hands trembled at the thought of touching him, but she drew a careful, steadying breath, and shut her mind to everything except the task of easing the tension out of his body. She poured the sweet-smelling oil into the palm of one hand, and rubbed her palms together lightly. Her heart bumped uncomfortably against her ribs, but she could no longer avoid touching him. His skin was warm beneath her hands and, concentrating at first on his neck and his shoulders, she slowly worked her way down his spine, her thumbs centred on the pressure points and her fingers kneading the taut muscles.

She sensed that his tension was not entirely due to the strain of the past two days. He was as aware of her as she was of him, and as a result the therapeutic massage was not as beneficial as it ought to be.

'Relax, Steve,' she ordered softly, keeping her voice low and calm. 'Please try to relax, or I might as well give up trying to help you.'

He grunted something into the pillow, and when she looked up, her glance fell on the radio built into the bedside cupboard. She switched it on, making sure the volume was low, and resumed her task as the relaxing, late-night music emerged from the hidden speakers.

It seemed to have the desired effect, and Loren

continued the massage as she felt Steve's muscles
relaxing beneath her fingers. She could hear him
breathing deeply and evenly as she worked her way up
towards his shoulders once more, and a smile of
satisfaction curved her mouth.

'Hm . . . that feels wonderful,' he murmured in a lazy,
relaxed voice. 'Where did you learn to do this sort of thing?'

'My father has an old back injury which frequently
causes him to suffer a great deal of pain, but my mother
is a trained nurse and a qualified masseuse,' Loren
explained, keeping her voice low. 'She taught me how
to do it in case she wasn't available when my father
needed help.'

He turned his head on the pillow so that she could
see his profile, and there was a lazy, relaxed smile on his
lips. 'She trained you well, Loren.'

Her fingers and her wrists were aching, but the
elasticity of his muscles told her she had done well.
'How does it feel?'

'Marvellous,' he grunted when she sat back with her
hands resting in her lap, and he rolled over on to his
back, his eyes faintly mocking beneath the now heavy
lids. 'Are you going to do my front as well?'

'If you think you need it,' she replied matter-of-
factly, despite the increased tempo of her pulse.

'I need it,' he assured her, making himself more
comfortable on the enormous bed.

'What you need is a holiday,' she argued quietly
above the mellow sound of the music, centring her
thumbs on his forehead, and working her way out
towards his temples and down along his tense jaw until
the muscles relaxed. 'You work too hard, Steve, and
you try to do too much on your own.'

'Habit dies hard,' he sighed, closing his eyes when she
expertly extended her therapeutic manipulations to his
neck, shoulders and chest.

'There's no sense in having a man with Jim MacDonald's potential working for you when you don't make use of him.'

'I suppose that's true.'

'Don't suppose, Steve,' she persisted gravely, loving the feel of his skin beneath her fingers. 'Consider it seriously.'

He raised his heavy eyelids and smiled faintly. 'I'll do whatever you say.'

'You're mocking me,' she accused crossly.

'Teasing,' he corrected lazily, staying the action of her hands, and pressing them against his chest so that the roughness of his hair was against her palms. 'There is a slight difference, you know.'

His eyes were a brilliant blue when they met hers, and the heavy, rhythmic beat of his heart was beneath her sensitive, aching fingers. An awareness flared between them which was sharp and sweet in its intensity, and little tremors of mingled fear and excitement raced through her. Steve raised his hands to the coiled knot at the back of her head and slowly began to remove the pins until the heavy mass of honey-gold hair tumbled down to her shoulders. He placed the pins on the bedside table without taking his eyes from hers, then he was running his fingers through her hair as if he enjoyed the feel of it.

'Steve . . .' his name passed her lips in something close to a plea, but his hand was beneath the glossy veil framing her flushed face, and his fingers were spread out against the back of her skull in a tingling, persuasive caress that brought her head down to his until his mouth closed over her parted, undeniably eager lips.

His mouth was warm and tasted slightly of whisky as it moved beneath hers in a lingering, sensual kiss, and it awakened a response in her which she could not suppress. Her fingers curled in an unintentional caress against his chest, and somehow the lack of urgency in his kiss drained away her fear to leave only the throbbing enjoyment of this timeless moment of intimacy between them. His hands worked their way through her hair and down her back, pressing her closer to his hard chest so that she could feel their hearts thudding in unison, but his hold on her relaxed eventually, and he eased her a little away from him.

'You're so beautiful, my Loren,' he murmured in a throaty, tired voice, and his fingers caressed her cheek and her throat tenderly rather than sensually. 'I want you so much, but I know I'd make a hash of it if I tried to make love to you now, and for you the first time has to be perfect.'

She raised a hand and brushed her fingers lightly over his heavy eyelids to force them shut. 'Go to sleep.'

'You're an angel,' he sighed, his features free of those visible lines of strain, and his body relaxed.

Loren sat there beside him for some time until his slow, shallow breathing told her that he was asleep. If she did not know that he was thirty-eight, she would at that moment have said he was ten years younger, and, as a rush of tender warmth invaded her, she raised his limp hand and pressed her lips lightly against his knuckles before she switched off the radio and the bedside light.

She left the room quietly and let herself out of the house, making sure that the latch was on when she closed the heavy front door behind her. It was a cool, dark night, but within her she was still nursing that warmth he had aroused, and it remained with her as she drove herself along the well-lit route to the centre of the city.

Loren slept late on Saturday morning, and throughout the day she found herself thinking almost continually about Steve. She thought about Lee as well, and wondered if she would ever hear the true facts of that incident which had occurred in China so many years ago.

Steve occupied her mind to such an extent that day that she was not entirely surprised when she opened the door that evening to find him standing on her doorstep. She could almost believe that her mind had conjured him up, but she found him very real when he pulled her into his arms and kissed her until she was trembling and breathless.

'I've spent the entire day thinking about what you said last night,' he told her, taking off his black leather jacket and lowering his muscular length into a chair.

'I said quite a few things last night,' she smiled, seating herself in a chair close by, and clasping her trembling hands tightly in her lap. 'What, in particular, are you referring to?'

'Well, firstly you said that I need a holiday, and secondly you suggested that I make better use of a man with Jim MacDonald's potential.'

'And thirdly?' she prompted, holding her breath for some reason she could not explain to herself when she saw that distinctly mocking smile curve his mouth.

'I'm going to take your advice.'

'You're going away on a holiday?' she asked, not quite sure whether she ought to feel delighted or disturbed at the thought of him going away for a time.

'I decided this morning that, as soon as I can get a flight to London, I'm going to pack my bags and spend six weeks touring the British Isles and Europe,' he enlightened her.

'That sounds lovely,' she forced a measure of enthusiasm into her voice, 'and you need the break away from work.'

'It would be ideal if you decide to come with me.'

His softly spoken words fell lightly on her ears, and

she stared at him blankly for several seconds before his invitation filtered through to her mind to make a stunning impact.

'Don't be silly,' she laughed in an attempt to brush aside a remark which could only have been made in jest.

'I'm serious,' he corrected her, his eyes narrowed and watchful. 'Come with me, Loren, and let me take you to the countries I've visited, and the places I've seen.'

Loren rose slowly to her feet and walked across to the window to stare down into the busy street below. She had a distinct feeling that someone was holding a knife to her heart, and one false move could pierce it. 'Come with me,' Steve had said, but what she could not decide was whether this was a proposition or a proposal.

'Are you asking me to come with you as your mistress?' she asked when she felt him come up behind her. He was standing so close to her that she could feel the heat of his body against her own, but his hands on her shoulders drew her back further until she was forced to lean against him while his lips caressed the nape of her neck and sent an unwanted shiver of pleasure through her.

'The French have a better expression for it,' he said, his voice deep and velvety soft against her ear. 'They call it *petite amie*.'

She felt the savage thrust of that threatening knife, she felt the agonising pain of the blade cutting deep, and in that moment something died within her to leave her cold and detached from this man she loved so much.

'*Petite amie!* Mistress!' She repeated the words distastefully as she turned beneath his hands and stepped a little away from him. 'Whichever word you choose to use, Steve, it means the same thing.'

'Loren, listen to me.' He reached for her, but she stepped beyond his reach once again and raised stormy eyes to his.

'And what happens when we return from this delightful holiday you've planned?' she demanded, an icy anger beginning to flow into her veins. 'Do we say "goodbye, it's been fun", and go our separate ways?'

'That will depend on how we feel about each other after spending every day of the next six weeks together,' he replied, and his blatant mockery fanned her anger into a white-hot flame.

'I can tell you right now how I feel about you without you having to wait that long,' she informed him with icy disdain. 'You disgust me!'

Steve was so arrogantly sure of himself and his powers of persuasion that he stared at her in disbelief for several seconds before he made another attempt to take her into his arms, but she moved away from him with such determination that he paused to study her with a quizzical look in his eyes.

'Loren?' he questioned, but this time the sound of her name on his lips did not arouse that melting sensation she had always experienced.

Her wits were sharpened by anger, and she sensed his determination even before he attempted to breach the gap between them once and for all. 'You're stronger than I am, Steve,' she warned in a choked voice, 'but if you lay a finger on me now I swear I'll be physically ill!'

He hesitated, his narrowed eyes speculative. 'I won't make this offer again, Loren, so I suggest you think it over.'

'No, *you* think it over!' she snapped. 'And I suggest you think along the lines of looking up one of those many women who call you so often on the telephone. I'm sure that among them you'll find someone eminently more suitable for what you have in mind!'

'I don't doubt that,' he barked harshly, slamming home the fact that he still had the power to hurt her, but she lowered her lashes to veil the pain in her eyes and turned from him.

'I knew you would agree with me,' she said in an icy, but controlled voice as she walked towards the door and opened it wide. 'Now, if you don't mind, I'd like you to leave.'

There was an undercurrent of crackling electricity in the air as they faced each other in silence, then Steve picked up his jacket and strode towards the door.

'I'll leave with pleasure!' he snarled as he passed her, then he wrenched the door from her hand so that the handle slipped from her fingers, and he slammed it shut behind him with a force that rattled the windows.

An icy calmness took possession of Loren as she slid the latch into place. In the mirror above the telephone her face looked white, and her eyes perhaps a little wild, but other than that her features were controlled. She could feel nothing, and it was as if her insides had turned to stone, but her mind was alert and totally rational. It was then, with no emotion to cloud her thoughts, that she made the only possible decision concerning her future.

Harvey Griffin took off his glasses, wiped the lenses on his handkerchief, and put his glasses on again. He cleared his throat, and tapped his fingers agitatedly on her letter of resignation which lay on the blotter in front of him. 'You can't give a week's notice, Miss Fraser!'

'Oh, yes, I can, Mr Griffin,' Loren contradicted him where she sat stiffly on the edge of her chair and faced him across his desk. 'It says so in my contract, if you would care to look it up.'

'But where am I going to find someone to take your place at such short notice?' he spluttered.

'That's your problem, not mine,' she snapped unkindly, but she felt ashamed of herself the next instant. 'I suggest you promote Natalie Miller into my position, and find someone else to take her place.'

He studied her thoughtfully for a moment, then nodded. 'Yes, I must admit she's quite capable.'

'I knew you'd think that,' Loren smiled without humour.

'Very well, Miss Fraser,' Harvey announced, filing her resignation. 'It seems I have no option but to accept your resignation.'

Loren thanked him politely and returned to her own office to resume her work, but, when Natalie walked in a half hour later, she pushed everything aside and gestured her into a chair.

'There's something I must tell you before you hear it elsewhere,' she said gravely. 'I've resigned, and next week Monday will be my last day here with Beaumont Engineering.'

Natalie's eyes widened in distress. 'You're not serious!'

'I'm afraid I am,' Loren assured her, and she was grateful for that frozen feeling inside of her which still left her devoid of feeling. 'I'm going home to Aberdeen where I belong.'

'But why?'

Loren lowered her gaze and said bitingly, 'You should know the answer that that question.'

'Steve Beaumont?' Natalie summed up the situation accurately.

'Yes,' Loren confirmed, the mention of his name sending the first stab of feeling through her since Saturday evening. 'I know it's cowardly of me, but I can't stay on here, Natalie. Not after ... not after what's happened between us.'

'I suppose if I asked for details you'd tell me to mind my own business?'

'I'd rather not talk about it,' Loren said abruptly, then she changed the subject. 'Your sister and brother-in-law return from their overseas trip on Sunday, so it all works out very nicely.'

'Where will you stay until you leave?' Natalie questioned her.

'I'll book into a hotel for the two nights.'

'Oh, no, you won't,' the younger girl announced. 'There's a spare bed in my room, and I insist you use it, or I shall never speak to you again.'

'I don't want to inconvenience——'

'Rubbish!' Natalie interrupted her fiercely. 'You're moving in with us for those two nights, and that's that!'

She stormed out of Loren's office without giving her the chance to argue, but Loren no longer had the desire to do so. She could not think of anything pleasanter than spending a little time with her friends before her departure, but in the interim there were still quite a few things she had to arrange. She had to telephone the agency to ask them to remove her name from their waiting list for a flat, and she had to start packing.

If she had been afraid that Steve might make an attempt to contact her again, then her fears had been quite unnecessary. She had no idea whether he still intended taking a holiday, but she did not particularly care what he did. He was at work every day that week, she had known this even though she had not seen him, and Mrs Markham was again very much in possession of her domain. Loren did, however, see Mrs Markham for a moment to speak to her, but their meeting had been brief, and Loren had not mentioned the fact that she was leaving, although she was certain that Mrs Markham and Steve were both aware of this.

She spent most of the Saturday tidying up the flat in order to leave it exactly the way she had found it, and above all she saw to it that the cupboards and the refrigerator would be well stocked when Caroline and her husband arrived the following morning.

She was persuaded to go out to the airport with Natalie and her mother on the Sunday morning to meet Caroline and Robert, and they all returned to the flat afterwards for tea. It gave Loren the opportunity to hand over the keys and to thank them for letting her use the flat, but as she saw the closeness between those two tanned and happy people it awakened a longing within her. She clamped it down fiercely, and allowed herself no time to dwell on that heavy feeling in her chest while she concentrated on the excited conversation around her.

Loren's last day at the office was a day like any other mainly because of her rigid self-control. She was not going to cry. There were, after all, no tears to shed. She had been foolish enough to fall in love with a man who had offered her no more than a temporary place in his life, but she was not going to be foolish enough to cry about it. It was over, and all she wanted to do was forget it ever happened. She would go home to the farm to help her father and, pray God, she was going to work Steve right out of her system.

'You don't know how I wish you didn't have to go,' Natalie said tearfully when she saw Loren off early on Tuesday morning, and Loren hugged her impulsively.

'You've been a wonderful friend, and I'll never forget you.'

She did not prolong her goodbyes, and she was heading south towards Aberdeen when the sun rose above the tall buildings. The Stanza's tank was full, but Loren's heart was empty, and when she pulled off the road later that morning for a break in her journey, she found herself releasing the tears which she had vowed not to shed. She despised herself for being so weak, but the tears flowed unrestrained, and they continued to flow for some time before she managed to control herself sufficiently to get out of the car to stretch her legs. She poured herself a cup of coffee from the flask and drank it quickly. Aberdeen was still a long way away, and if she was going to waste precious minutes every time she stopped to bawl her eyes out, then she was not going to get there before dark.

She travelled most of the day at a steady pace, stopping only occasionally to stretch her legs, or when the hot sun made her drowsy. She shut her mind to everything except reaching her destination, and somehow she succeeded. Her arrival at the farm was not going to be a surprise to her parents. She had sent them a telegram the day before to let them know they could expect her for dinner that evening, or a little later, and when she entered Karoo country late that afternoon, her foot went down a little heavier on the accelerator. It was not far now to Aberdeen; sixty kilometres was a mere nothing compared to the distance she had already travelled that day, and, despite her impatience, her tired eyes scanned the arid land with an almost tender affection.

Will and Jean Fraser were sitting out on the wide front verandah when Loren drove up to the house at sunset, and they welcomed her enthusiastically, but also a little curiously. They helped her to carry her suitcases from the car into the house, laughing and talking almost simultaneously about how excited they had been to receive her telegram. If they noticed that Loren was strangely quiet, then they made no mention of it, and after a long cool drink to quench her thrist, she left them out on the verandah to go and take a shower and change into something fresh for dinner.

It was good to be home with all the familiar things surrounding her, but a part of her would always yearn for that *something* unobtainable which was now so far removed from her.

'I must say your father and I never expected to have you back here with us so soon,' her mother remarked at the dinner table an hour later, broaching the subject of her return for the first time.

'I was homesick,' Loren evaded the truth with a little lie, 'and Johannesburg wasn't exactly the best place to be.'

Not while Steve was there, she could have added, but she remained stoically silent about that part of her life which was now behind her.

'What are you going to do now?' her father wanted to know, and she shrugged with affected casualness.

'I thought I might help you on the farm for a while before I start looking for something else.'

Will Fraser studied his daughter in thoughtful silence for a moment. He knew there was something wrong, she could see that, but he would not pry, and a smile creased his rugged face. 'I could do with some help,' he admitted.

Loren fairly threw herself into the work on the farm, doing anything and everything she could lay her hands on, and not sparing herself for one moment. She could forget during the day while she toiled in the hot sun, but at night she remembered every agonising detail of why she had left Johannesburg. She had said she despised Steve, that he disgusted her, but in her heart she knew that she still loved him, and she would go on loving him for the rest of her life.

If Steve had said just once that he loved her she would have thrown away everything she held most dear, and she would have followed him to the ends of the earth, she realised one star-studded night when she had been home three weeks. It was too hot to sleep. She was restless in the face of her mental agony, and she went out on to the darkened verandah for a breath of fresh air. She felt exhausted, but her mind would not let her rest, and her longing was like a physical pain in her breast. 'Oh, God!' she groaned inwardly, leaning against the rail and burying her face in her hands. 'Am I never going to forget him?'

'Tired?' her father asked behind her, startling her into an upright position.

'Yes, I am,' she replied, and that was not entirely a lie. She was tired of the aching emptiness within her, and she was tired of the lonely hours at night when her thoughts of Steve kept her awake to the extent that she had to face the following day with deep shadows beneath her eyes.

'Something happened in Johannesburg, didn't it?' said Will, leaning against the rail beside her while he lit his pipe. 'Something happened, and you're unhappy because of it.'

Loren raised her glance towards the stars and listened to the familiar sound of a jackal howling in the distance. 'I don't want to talk about it.'

'Is that why you're working as if the devil himself is chasing you?' her father persisted.

'It helps to keep myself busy,' she heard herself confessing only partly to being unhappy.

'It stops you from thinking too much, doesn't it?'

'Yes, it does.'

'But when you stand here alone in the dark at night you make up for all the hours during the day,' he shrewdly hit on the very basis of her existence.

'Oh, Dad!' she croaked, fighting desperately against the desire to burst into tears.

'It sometimes helps to talk,' he assured her, putting away his pipe and placing a comforting arm about her slim shoulders.

'No,' she whispered, leaning her head against him. 'It still hurts too much to talk about it.'

'Well, when you're ready,' he said, kissing her on the forehead. 'Your mother and I will be waiting to listen and help where we can.'

'I know . . . and thank you,' she sighed heavily, and they stood close together like that for some time before he moved away from her to go inside.

'Don't stay out too long,' he advised. 'It still gets chilly late at night.'

Alone in the darkness again with only the night sounds for company, Loren found herself wondering what Steve was doing at that moment. Did he go on holiday as he had planned to, and did he take someone else with him? The thought of another woman in his arms sent a fresh stab of pain through her. Her eyes filled rapidly with tears, and the stars danced crazily in the dark, velvety sky. There was no sense in punishing herself this way, she knew that, but her mind would not be stilled, and the tears continued to race each other down her cheeks until she went inside and stumbled into bed to fall asleep from sheer exhaustion.

Loren arrived home late one afternoon after a particularly gruelling day in the shearing camp, and she stamped some of the dust off her boots before opening the screen door and entering the kitchen where her mother was stirring the stew on the stove. Jean glanced up when the screen door banged shut behind Loren, and her glance took in her dusty denims and sweat-stained shirt without remarking upon it.

'There's a letter for you from Johannesburg,' she said, putting down the ladle and placing the lid on the pot. 'I put it on the bedside table in your room.'

'Thanks,' Loren smiled briefly, looking outwardly calm, but inwardly her nerves had coiled themselves into a tight knot.

The letter would be from Natalie. She had promised she would write, but Loren somehow feared the contents. There would be news in it about Beaumont Engineering, and that was a part of her life which she was trying desperately to forget.

Loren went up to her room, and it was as she had suspected. The letter was from Natalie, she recognised that small, neat handwriting and, despite everything, a smile of pleasure curved her mouth. She would shower and change first, and after that she might have sufficient courage to read it.

Since returning to Aberdeen she had seen Matt Kruger a few times, and they had slipped back into that easy relationship they had enjoyed once before while she had still worked for him. He had questioned her return to the farm after being away a little more than three months, but he had not pressed her for an explanation. After almost four weeks back at home the rumours had begun to circulate once again amongst old friends and acquaintances, but this time the speculations about her relationship with Matt did not touch Loren.

She shed her grimy clothes and pulled off her dusty boots, and when she stood beneath the cool jet of water in the shower she tried to shut her mind to everything except the pleasure of cooling off her heated body, and soaping away the dust. The clouds were building up perfectly and, with a little luck, it would rain during the night. The drought was easing, and now, as they approached the end of September, the veld was coming alive again. They had had their first spring showers, but they needed a good downpour before the farmers in the district would be able to hold their heads high again.

Loren washed her hair in the shower, and twisted a towel about her head before she stepped out of the cubicle to drape a bath sheet about her damp body. She brushed her teeth, and studied herself critically in the mirror above the basin when she had rinsed out her mouth. Sleepless nights might have put permanent

shadows beneath her eyes, but the many working and
leisure hours in the Karoo sun had tanned her body
until it was a golden brown all over except where her
bikini covered her. She looked healthy, and she looked
relaxed, but inside there was still that aching emptiness
which nothing and no one could fill. She had lost
weight, but with less to do and more time to think she
might have lost more, and she could not thank her
father enough for passing so many of his tasks on to
her.

She changed eventually into a cool cotton frock and
sandals, but only when she had applied a little make-up
and had dried and brushed her hair did she sit down on
her bed to open Natalie's letter. Natalie had filled three
pages mainly with the amusing and interesting incidents
which had occurred to Caroline and Robert during
their trip, but towards the end of the letter Loren
encountered the news she had feared from the start.

'I saw Mrs Markham the other day and, for a change,
she was actually quite nice,' Natalie had written. 'She was
so concerned about the chief that I don't suppose it really
mattered to her to whom she was speaking, and she let out
quite a few interesting facts. The chief has been driving
himself so hard lately that she fears he'll have a
breakdown or something drastic. When he's not away on
business, he's working late at the office, and he almost
collapsed in her office one afternoon. Can you imagine it?
The chief said it must have been something he ate for
lunch, but Mrs Markham seems to think differently. I tell
you, the woman is almost demented with worry, and I
must admit that when I caught sight of him a few days ago
he didn't look so good.'

Natalie ended her letter there with the usual good
wishes, and Loren lowered it on to her lap while she
stared straight ahead of her with unseeing eyes. So
Steve had not gone away for a holiday and taken some

woman with him. That should have been of some comfort to her, but instead she found herself troubled by his obvious unconcern for his own health.

Why was he driving himself so hard? What was he trying to do to himself? She could not find an answer to these queries, and it was doubtful if anyone would ever completely understand a man like Steve Beaumont. She wished she could help him, but she did not think he would welcome her proffered assistance. They had said too many hurtful things to allow for an easy relationship, and the only relationship Steve would be interested in was one without commitments.

She tried to thrust aside the disturbing information she had received from Natalie, but during the next few days she found herself becoming increasingly concerned. Steve might have thrust her out of his mind and his life, but that did not stop her from caring.

CHAPTER TEN

IT rained for two days as if the sluice gates in the sky had been opened, and a deluge of water swept across the parched earth, filling the dams and uprooting thorn trees. There was nothing they could do about the damage until the torrential rain ceased, and when it did, Loren was out there working alongside her father to repair the fences which had been damaged. Will Fraser, like everyone else, counted his losses, but it was a small price to pay for the much-needed rain they had received.

They worked almost night and day to restore order, and they arrived home late on the Friday evening in a truck which had stalled twice along the way, but Jean Fraser had kept their food warm in the oven as she had done most nights since the storm.

'I'll have to overhaul the truck some time,' Loren's father grunted when they sat down to their meal at the kitchen table.

'I'll take a look at it tomorrow,' Loren promised.

'Can't it wait until Monday?' her mother protested. 'You've worked hard all week, and you deserve to have the weekend free to relax.'

'We need that truck on Monday to fetch supplies in town,' Loren reminded her mother, and Jean sighed resignedly as she turned away to pour their coffee.

Loren felt exhausted when she went upstairs half an hour later, and after a hot bath she crawled into bed. For the first time in weeks she did not lie awake for hours, and she went to sleep almost the minute her head touched the pillow.

The sun had not yet risen the following morning when Loren was up and dressed in a clean pair of blue denims and checked shirt. She toasted a slice of bread and made herself a cup of coffee in the kitchen, and the rising sun was only just beginning to set fire to the eastern hills when she left the house and walked across to the barn where they had parked the truck the night before. The dew glistened like diamonds on the grass, and it added that familiar sparkle to the Karoo morning. Loren breathed the air deep into her lungs, and she caught the faint but distinctive scent of the Karoo bush. It was good to be alive, but her life would only be complete if . . .!

She brought her thoughts to an abrupt halt. She had to stop thinking about Steve; she had to forget! But deep down in her heart she knew that she would never be able to forget him entirely. He would always remain a part of her no matter where she was, or what she was doing, and she would simply have to learn to live with that knowledge.

The barn door creaked and swung open beneath her hand, and the pale sunlight slanted in to give her sufficient light when she raised the bonnet of the truck. She cast an experienced eye over the interior, and found the fault without much difficulty. It would take no more than two hours at the most to repair it, but before she did so she loosened the required plugs to drain out the oil. She cleaned the engine thoroughly and poured in fresh oil from the stock which her father kept on a shelf in the barn. With the necessary equipment close at hand, she slid beneath the truck again, and she was still there almost two hours later when she heard heavy footsteps approaching the barn. They halted a few paces away from her, and a smile of amusement curved her mouth.

'You've come too late to help me, Dad, but if you

pass me that small spanner I'll be finished in a moment.' She held out her hand, the spanner was placed in it, and she tightened the nut securely before she slid out from the under the truck. 'Well, that should do it.'

Loren was still down there on the dusty concrete floor when she caught sight of polished leather shoes which were definitely not the kind her father usually wore about the farm. Her glance shifted higher, taking in the expensive material of the dark brown pants that covered the long, muscular limbs, and a crocodile-skin belt hugged the pants firmly about a slim waist. The cream-coloured silk shirt was unbuttoned at the throat, and her heart felt as if it were beating in her mouth long before she found herself staring up into those achingly familiar blue eyes.

'Steve!' she gasped, scrambling to her feet without his assistance and leaning heavily against the truck when it felt as if her legs would not hold her in an upright position.

His smile was twisted and faintly cynical as he appraised her and drawled, 'Hello, Loren.'

She was suddenly painfully aware of her appearance. Her hair was tied back from her face in a ponytail, her face was devoid of make-up, and her denims and shirt looked as if she had been sprinkled with grease and oil and dust. She forgot about her own appearance, however, when she took a closer look at Steve. There was an unfamiliar hint of grey in his hair against his temples, and his eyes had a glazed look about them as if they were not properly focussed. He had lost weight, she could see it in the way his skin seemed to stretch too tightly across his high cheekbones, and when his smile faded she felt a painful wrench at her heart when she saw his grim, drawn expression.

'You look as if you haven't slept all night,' she

observed, her voice husky with the effort to control her clamouring emotions.

'As a matter of fact I haven't,' he confessed, his glance holding hers. 'I decided late yesterday afternoon to take this trip down here, and I drove through the night.'

'You've been up at the house?' she asked with an oddly breathless feeling in her chest, and he nodded briefly.

'Your mother very kindly gave me breakfast when I arrived, and I've spent more than an hour talking to your parents.'

'Oh,' she said, that breathless feeling intensifying when she saw something close to an accusation in his eyes.

'You never told them about me.'

'No,' she answered abruptly, turning from him to slam down the bonnet of the truck, and to wipe her hands on a cloth. 'I saw no reason to enlighten them about my senseless involvement with you.'

'It took quite some time explaining who I was, and why I'd come.'

Her back went rigid, and the breath seemed to still in her throat. 'Why did you come?'

He came up behind her, but fortunately he made no attempt to touch her, or she might have made a complete fool of herself by flinging herself into his arms in her desperate need to feel close to him again.

'I came hoping to persuade you to come back to Johannesburg with me,' he explained, and Loren closed her eyes momentarily. She waited for something which she knew would not come, and she hated herself for it. Steve wanted her back in Johannesburg as his mistress, and she was fool enough to have hoped for something more than that.

'Get in,' she said tritely, wrenching open the door on

the driver's side and climbing into the truck. 'I have to give it a run to check it.'

Steve got in beside her, and the truck's engine roared when she turned the key in the ignition. Neither of them spoke as she drove out of the barn and she took the road leading up on to a little hill from where one had an excellent view of the farm. She could not explain why she was taking him there, but when she parked the truck on the crest of the hill she jumped out and walked a few paces away to let her narrowed glance slide over the sundrenched veld that stretched far into the distance.

She was aware of Steve coming up behind her, but she was aware also of the wounds his presence had ripped open. Oh, God, why did he have to come here? she thought. Why does he have to torture me like this?

'Loren . . .'

'I should never have gone to Johannesburg,' she forestalled him, releasing some of the misery she had carried around within her these past weeks. 'People think and feel differently there from the way they do here. Right is right, and wrong is still wrong here, but in Johannesburg it's quite the opposite. I can't accept that, and I never will, so I've come to the conclusion that this is where I belong.'

'You belong with me!' he exlaimed harshly, his hands on her shoulders swinging her round roughly so that he could look down into her pale face with the smear of grease across one cheek, but she shook her head.

'No, Steve, I don't belong with you.'

'Yes, you do!' he contradicted her emphatic denial to his statement, and his eyes were like blue fire now as they blazed down into hers. 'I've been to hell and back these past weeks. I tried to tell myself that you're not worth bothering a scrap about, but that didn't help me to forget you. I looked up all those women you mentioned, and I took a different one out almost every night, but they all had your eyes, your mouth, your voice, and your hair.' He groaned and his hands fell to his sides to hang there limply from his sagging shoulders. 'They must have thought I'd gone mad when I said a polite "Goodnight" to them on their doorsteps without so much as shaking hands!'

'Steve . . .'

'When I couldn't build up a spark of enthusiasm for any of those women, I buried myself in my work' he continued as if she had not spoken. 'It helped, but only up to a point. The more hours I put in, the more I thought about you, and in the end I had to face up to the fact that without you Beaumont Engineering could fall apart at the seams for all I cared. Nothing made sense without you there to share my life with me, or to bully me into doing things, and I don't know why I hadn't realised that before.'

He was tearing away at the armour she had placed about her heart, but she was determined not to read too much into what he was saying.

'Come on,' Loren said abruptly when she saw him swaying on his feet. That glazed look was back in his eyes and, sliding a supporting arm about his waist, she walked him towards the truck. 'You're just about asleep on your feet.'

'You smell of grease and cologne,' he smiled down into her veiled eyes when she had opened the door on the passenger side of the truck for him. 'It's quite a delightful mixture!'

'Get in!' she ordered sharply, dangerously aware now of his hard body against her own, and he obeyed her surprisingly enough without putting up an argument.

'Loren . . .' he murmured her name in that deep-throated voice which would always have the power to stir her senses, but she had no intention of letting him say something which he might regret afterwards.

'Don't say another word,' she begged. 'We'll talk later.'

Steve sighed heavily and stretched out his long legs as far as the interior of the truck would allow. He closed his eyes, but she knew he was not asleep during the short drive back to the house where his tomato-red Jaguar stood parked in the shade of a willow tree.

Jean Fraser was in the hall when they entered the house, and she glanced strangely at Loren before her trained eyes recognised the fatigue of the man who had walked into the house with her daughter.

'I've put your things in the guest room, Mr Beaumont, if you would like to go upstairs and rest,' she told him with a warm smile to which he responded.

'That's very kind of you, Mrs Fraser,' he thanked her. 'I could do with a few hours' sleep.'

'Loren will show you the way,' Jean told him, and as they approached the stairs, Loren glanced back at her mother, to catch a glimpse of that extraordinary expression in her eyes once again.

What had Steve told her parents? she wondered frantically while she led the way up to the guest room. What, for the love of heaven, had he told them?

Her mind was in such a flat spin that she nearly leapt out of her skin at the sound of her name on Steve's lips, and she glanced about her a little wildly for a moment to discover that they were standing beside the bed in the spacious guest room.

'Lie down, and loosen your belt,' she said briskly, her hands against his wide chest pushing him back so that he sat down rather heavily on the well-sprung bed.

His hands went to the buckle of his belt, but his glazed eyes sought hers and held her glance until he lifted his legs on to the bed and lay back against the pillows. Her face felt stiff with the effort to hide her feelings when she unlaced his shoes and placed them on the floor beside the bed. She had to get away from him, she could not bear it a moment longer to be this close to him and yet so far away, but his hand reached out to grip hers as if he had sensed her desire to flee from him.

'Don't go away,' he pleaded, and although his voice was slurred with tiredness, his strength was unimpaired when he tugged at her hand and forced her to sit down beside him.

'I'll be here when you wake up,' she heard herself saying in a stilted voice, and her fingers curled about his of their own volition.

'Is that a promise?'

That hint of anxiety in his eyes stabbed directly into her soul, and her throat tightened, forcing her to swallow convulsively. 'It's a promise.'

He relaxed visibly, and his heavy eyelids drooped, but his hand still gripped hers tightly, and it was a long time before his hold relaxed. He was breathing deeply and evenly in his sleep, and Loren's hungry glance roamed his beloved features at will, taking in once again the strange hollowness in his cheeks, and the lines of strain which seemed to have become permanently etched about his mouth and eyes. He looked so oddly vulnerable lying there that a choking tenderness surged through her, and she made no attempt to brush away the hot tears blurring her vision.

'I love you, Steve. No matter what you are, and no matter what you do, I shall always love you,' she whispered softly, but he was sleeping too deeply to hear her, and she brushed her quivering lips against the back of his hand before she lowered it to the bed and rose carefully to her feet.

She went out and closed the door quietly behind her, but when she turned she found herself confronted by her mother, and there was no time to hide the tears in her eyes.

'Is he asleep?' Jean asked in a lowered voice.

'Yes,' Loren whispered, making a desperate attempt to control her tears, but they continued to flow down her cheeks. 'Oh, Mother!'

'I know,' Jean murmured, sliding a comforting arm about Loren's shoulders and leading her towards the stairs. 'It hurts to love someone like that.'

Her mother was shrewd, much shrewder than Loren had imagined, and she did not deny the truth when she realised there was no longer any sense in hiding her feelings.

'What I need now is a strong cup of tea,' Loren said unsteadily when they entered the kitchen.

'I think we both need a strong cup of tea,' her mother agreed, switching on the kettle. 'And after that I suggest you take a bath and change into something pretty.'

Loren's smile was shaky, but deeply amused as she sat down at the table and slanted a glance at her mother. She had a pretty good idea of how she looked. She was dusty and grimy after the hours spent working on the truck, and this was how Steve had found her. It horrified her now to think of it, but she could also see the humorous side of it, and it was a relief to know that her sense of humour was still intact after everything that had happened to her.

Jean Fraser smiled down into her daughter's amused eyes, and Loren saw there an understanding far deeper than she had imagined. It had been wrong of her, perhaps, not to take her parents into her confidence, but even now she found it difficult to voice her feelings for Steve, and the fears which accompanied her love for him.

Loren went upstairs again half an hour later and paused for a moment in the passage outside the guest

room before going on to her own bedroom. 'I came
hoping to persuade you to come back to Johannesburg
with me,' his words later ricocheted through her mind
while she bathed and washed her hair. What exactly
had he meant by that? Was he going to come forward
with the same proposition he had made to her before?

'Oh, God, no, *no*! I couldn't bear it!' she groaned
inwardly as she stepped out of the bath.

She wrapped the bath sheet around her damp body,
and leaned against the bathroom wall for a moment to
ease that stabbing ache that seared through her. She
had only just begun to imagine that she could live
without Steve, but seeing him again had made her
realise how stupid she had been in thinking that she
could ever really forget him.

'I've been to hell and back these past weeks,' he had
told her. 'I tried to tell myself that you're not worth
bothering a scrap about, but that didn't help me to
forget you.'

Was that true? Could she believe him? That haunted,
almost wild expression in his eyes had been convincing
enough. But did she dare imagine that he cared
sufficiently to come to her with a proposal on this
occasion instead of a proposition which she could never
accept?

She changed into a floral silk frock with a touch of
gold in it that matched the gold in her tawny eyes, and
when she had dried her hair she brushed it with a
vigour that matched her disturbing thoughts. She
applied a touch of make-up to her face, and was
surprised to see she was a little pale beneath her newly
acquired tan. With a comfortable pair of sandals on her
feet, she checked her appearance briefly in the mirror,
then went downstairs to join her parents for tea.

Her father had tea with them on the wide, shady
verandah, and although he mentioned Steve briefly, he

centred the discussion mostly on his hopes for the future after the good rains they had received. Loren was grateful for this, it gave her more time to compose herself for the inevitable confrontation between Steve and herself, but she admitted to herself that she was not looking forward to it.

Steve did not come down for lunch. It was best to let him sleep, Jean advised, and no one contradicted her wisdom in such matters. Loren sat about aimlessly on the cool verandah after lunch when her parents went up to their room to rest for an hour, but she could no longer contain her restlessness when Steve had not awakened by four o'clock that afternoon.

'I'm going for a walk,' she said, her expression guarded when she met her parents' curious glances. 'I'll be down at the old well if I'm needed.'

She walked away from the house with the hot sun beating down on her face and her arms, but she paused beyond the garden beneath the shade of the cypress and gum trees. She leaned against the stone wall of the well which was no longer in use, but her glance was restless and agitated as it shifted across the distant veld where the sheep were grazing so leisurely in the heat of the late afternoon sun. The cicadas shrilled loudly in the trees around her, and she waved away a bee that darted about her head, but her mind was in too much of a turmoil to take in her surroundings. She felt like a record player with the needle bouncing repeatedly over the same groove, and the refrain that echoed mercilessly through her brain was 'Steve, Steve, Steve!'

Loren had no idea how long she stood there, but the sun was setting swiftly when the sound of footsteps alerted her to the fact that she was no longer alone, and she turned warily to see Steve walking towards her. He had changed into blue denim pants and shirt, and that vital masculinity was reaching out to her again, but that hollowness in his cheeks and that strangely haunted look in his eyes was still clearly evident. He leaned against the wall beside her, and his nearness set her nerves vibrating in a most alarming way.

'Is this actually a well?' he asked, peering down into the darkness.

'It used to be a well in earlier days, but now it's simply ornamental,' she told him, observing his features closely. 'Feeling better?'

'I feel like a new man after seven hours' sleep,' he smiled faintly, his eyes meeting hers with a probing intensity that made her look away hastily for fear of what he might see.

'There's a storm brewing again,' she said, casting her glance up at the distant sky. 'I can smell it in the air.'

'There's a storm brewing in me too,' he said quietly, and her heart quickened its pace as she turned to face him.

'You said a lot of things this morning——'

'And I meant every word,' he interrupted her gravely, his glance sliding over the golden sheen of her hair, and settling finally on her rigidly composed features.

'Let's walk,' she suggested, her heart pounding painfully in her breast, but his hand on her shoulder stopped her before she could move a pace away from him.

'What are you afraid of, Loren?'

She stared up into his eyes contemplatively, loving his touch, yet hating it for what it did to her, then she shrugged off his hand and walked a little distance away from him to where the trees were beginning to cast a deeper shade in the swiftly setting sun.

'I'm afraid of you,' she confessed with unavoidable honesty. 'I'm afraid of the way you make me feel, but most of all, I think, I'm afraid of being hurt.'

'I don't want to hurt you, Loren, incredible as that may seem to you.' He fell into step beside her as she walked on, but made no attempt to touch her again.

'My main purpose in coming here is to plead with you, if necessary, to give me the opportunity to rectify my past blunders'

How could he rectify the fact that he wanted her only as a mistress? He had made it quite clear from the beginning that a wife would simply be a nuisance, had he not? She steeled herself against the hurt and gestured towards the path leading off towards the right. 'If we walk this way we can watch the sun set behind those hills.'

Steve walked beside her in silence, but she was aware of him with every fibre of her being, and she cursed herself silently for still finding that aura of masculinity which surrounded him so appealing. If it were only his physical attributes which attracted her, then she might have been able to forget him, but it went far deeper than that. She loved him for the man he was; for his seemingly endless vitality, and for the gentle side to his often ruthless nature which he kept so well hidden. She thought of the Chinese, Lee, with the scarred face. His admiration and respect for Steve had been clearly evident in his dark, slanted eyes and Loren had no doubt that Lee would serve his employer devotedly for the rest of his life. A life for a life, that was obviously the creed by which Lee lived, and Loren could understand it. Would she not gladly devote the rest of her life to making Steve happy if he would only give her the opportunity she was seeking?

The sun dipped behind the hills. It was a red, fiery half moon which became smaller with every second, and then it disappeared. Its rays were still tinting the sky a delicate, glowing pink, and Loren sighed audibly without actually realising it.

'That was beautiful, wasn't it?' she asked softly, almost afraid to disturb the peaceful silence in the gathering dusk.

'Loren, look at me.'

The moment of complete honesty had come, but she shied away from it in fear. 'Please, Steve, can't it wait a——'

'Look at me!' he ordered in a quiet, insistent voice as he took her by the shoulders and forced her to face him, but she could not raise her glance higher than the brown column of his throat. 'If I can help it at all, then I don't want to watch another sunset or sunrise without you there to watch it with me. Do you understand what I'm saying?'

She raised her eyes to his at last, and what she saw there made the blood drum a little faster through her veins, but she had lived too long without hope to take anything at face value. 'Are you asking me to live with you?'

'I know that without you my life has no purpose, so what I'm seeking is a "till death us do part" arrangement.' His hands slid from her shoulders and up beneath the silken cloud of honey-gold hair to frame her face. 'I'm asking you to marry me, Loren.'

The most incredible joy burst from somewhere within her like the wall of a dam breaking to release its contents, but her eyes remained veiled beneath the intensity of his probing, pleading glance. 'In my book marriage is for ever, and if you're not absolutely sure that this is what you want, then "for ever" could become an agonising eternity.'

'I love you, Loren, and I need you,' he said the words she had longed to hear, and his deep-throated voice was vibrating with an emotion she had never heard before as he gazed deeply into her wary eyes. 'An eternity would be too short a time for me to prove it to you,' he added huskily.

The barriers were down, the masks were removed, and the most indescribable happiness swept through Loren.

In his eyes she saw her own feelings reflected as if she was looking into a mirror, and there was fear as well, a fear of having to fall back into that lonely, empty pit which life had been these past weeks.

'Oh, Steve!' she sighed tremulously, swaying towards him, and she felt the hard warmth of his arms about her as she buried her face against his broad chest.

'Does this mean you'll marry me?' he asked with a touching uncertainty which did not belong with this arrogant man, and she raised her glowing face to his to let him see into the hidden recesses of her soul.

'Yes, I'll marry you,' she whispered, her eyes filling with tears of happiness as she flung her arms about his waist and pressed her body closer to his. 'Oh, yes, please!'

His arms tightened about her almost convulsively, but when he lowered his lips to hers he kissed her with a lingering tenderness which stirred her more deeply than anything else had ever done before. This man loved her, and she no longer doubted it. Their kiss deepened with a mutual hunger for more, and it felt to her as if time itself stood still in that moment as their hearts beat in unison.

They remained there for a long time until the shadow deepened almost into darkness. When they finally drew apart Loren was flushed and trembling, and so deliriously happy that her heart felt as if it wanted to burst.

'How long are you staying?' she asked, dreading the thought of him going away from her as they walked hand in hand back to the house.

'I've been invited to stay until our wedding next Saturday.'

'Next Saturday?' she echoed weakly, pausing to stare up at him, and wondering how on earth she was going to be ready in time if he was absolutely serious.

'I have a fantastic honeymoon lined up for us.' A

devilish gleam entered his eyes. 'It's a six-week tour of the British Isles and Europe.'

His reminder of that hateful proposition he had once made sent the blood rushing into her cheeks, and her throat tightened with the memory of the agony she had suffered. 'Be serious, Steve!' she begged.

'I am serious,' he assured her now with unmistakable gravity. 'One trip into Aberdeen will be sufficient to make the necessary arrangements for our wedding, and a telephone call to Mrs Markham will see to it that our tickets for the flight to London will be ready and waiting for us when we arrive in Johannesburg.'

She stared up at him in silence for a moment, then a spark of amusement lit her eyes. 'I have a horrible feeling that I have no say in this matter!'

'Of course you have,' he mocked her. 'You can decide which country you'd like to visit first.'

'Oh, come on!' she laughed, tugging at his hand. 'Let's go up to the house.'

Will and Jean were sitting out on the darkened verandah, and seeing them made Loren stop abruptly to confront Steve. 'What did you tell my parents this morning when you spent that hour with them?'

'I told them that I was the imbecile who'd hurt you so badly, but that I wanted to marry you,' he smiled tightly. 'I asked them if they thought I stood a chance.'

'What did they say?' she asked, holding her breath.

'They didn't think there was much hope for me, but they gave me their blessing to go ahead and ask you. If I failed your father promised he'd give me a bottle of whisky to drown my sorrows in.' He smiled down at her with mock regret. 'That reminds me, I'm now minus a bottle of whisky!'

'Oh, you're being utterly impossible, and——' Loren halted her playful rebuke when she saw the laughter leave his eyes, and it was replaced by a smouldering look that made her tremble inwardly. 'I love you, Steve.'

'I should have known you'd choose a moment like this to say you love me when everyone is sitting out there on the verandah watching us,' he grimaced.

'I've never considered you a man to be put off your stride by an audience,' she mocked him, but she regretted it the next instant when a dangerous light leapt into his eyes.

'My God, you asked for this!' he warned and, regardless of their audience, he swept her into his arms and kissed her so thoroughly that she was flushed and breathless, and decidedly weak at the knees, when he finally released her.

Loren fastened the belt of her silk robe about her waist and turned from the open suitcase on the floor to finger the soft petals of the white chrysanthemums and carnations which had been arranged in a vase on the dressing table. The flowers had awaited them on their arrival late that afternoon, and they had been accompanied by a congratulatory card from Mrs Markham.

A happy smile curved Loren's mouth as she turned from the flowers and strolled idly across to the window to stare down into the garden of Steve's Houghton home. On the third finger of her left hand she felt the unfamiliar weight of a gold, intricately carved wedding band, and she still found it almost too incredible to believe that she was actually Steve's wife. It had been a hectic week, and an equally hectic day, but her wedding day was one she would remember and cherish for the rest of her life. Her parents had had the opportunity to get to know Steve, and they were content and happy with her choice.

Natalie and her mother had travelled down to attend

the wedding ceremony that morning, and Matt had also been there to make it a perfect occasion. To save time Steve had arranged for his Jaguar and Loren's Stanza to be railed up to Johannesburg, and he had chartered a flight from Aberdeen to Port Elizabeth. They had to wait an hour at the Port Elizabeth airport before their flight left for Johannesburg, but the purpose of it all was so that they could spend their wedding night in Steve's home before they flew to London on the Sunday afternoon. Their honeymoon was going to be six weeks of absolute bliss, Loren was certain of that, and she knew that Steve desperately needed this break away from his responsibilities.

The bathroom door opened a few minutes later, and she turned to see Steve combing his damp hair in front of the mirror. He had a towel draped about his lean hips, and his naked torso conjured up visions of that night she had given him a massage. What had followed was weeks of misery thinking he could never care for her, but that was all in the past now, and it made her appreciate her happiness at that moment so much more.

She walked up behind him and slid her arms about his waist. She pressed closer to that muscled back, and he moved slightly so that their eyes met in the dressing table mirror. He smiled at her, and he looked more like the man she used to know than the haggard human being who had confronted her on the farm a week ago. Loren smiled back at him with her heart in her eyes, and she brushed her lips against the smooth skin stretched across his shoulder. His stomach muscles hardened beneath her hands, then he turned in her arms and slid his hands down her back to mould her more firmly against his hard body.

The heat of his hands through her robe inflamed her, and his smouldering eyes held hers for a moment before he lowered his head to tantalise her lips with little kisses that made her hunger for more.

'Lee won't have dinner ready for another two hours,' he said throatily against her lips.

'That should give us plenty of time,' she whispered the bold invitation which stemmed from the sharp, sweet stab of desire that surged through her.

'My sentiments exactly,' he laughed softly as he slid her robe off her shoulders. It fell to the floor and remained there when he lifted her in his arms and carried her towards the bed with the lovers carved into the wooden headboard. She was shy initially when his eyes devoured her nakedness, but when he lay down beside her she was aware only of his tenderness, and the love that burned deep in his eyes before he lowered his head to slide his lips from her throat to her breast. 'You're so soft,' he murmured in that deep velvety voice that never failed to arouse her senses. 'And you smell like a fresh mountain breeze.'

'Oh, Steve, I love you so much,' she sighed ecstatically, locking her fingers in his mahogany hair, and after that she was totally lost in the storm of emotion that swept through her.

She was conscious only of his fiery lips and hands arousing her to a fever pitch of desire she had never known before, and, in the final giving of herself, he initiated her into that unknown and intense sphere of ecstasy that left her exhausted but wholly satisfied.

'I adore you, my sweet, beautiful darling,' Steve murmured long afterwards when they still lay with their bodies entwined as if they could not bear to be parted. 'Have I told you that yet today?'

'Yes, you have,' she sighed with a contented smile on her lips and a dreaminess in her eyes which he had put there. 'But I still find it almost too incredible to believe, so I don't mind hearing it again.'

'I was a blind, crass idiot. I valued my freedom so much that it finally became my prison, and I had to go through hell before I would face up to the truth,' he growled, his eyes darkening with an anger directed at himself as he brushed the golden strands of hair away from her flushed face, and his touch was infinitely tender. 'I'd go through hell for you again, Loren, but I never again want to hurt you the way I did.'

He meant it; he would never again deliberately hurt her, but she could not bear to see that haunted look in his eyes and she drew his head down until it came to rest against her breast. He sighed and tightened his arms about her slim, yielding body, and in that moment he was not only her lover, but her child. They belonged together, fate had decreed so from their first meeting, and it would remain so until eternity.

A WORD ABOUT THE AUTHOR

Yvonne Whittal grew up in South Africa, spending her summers on the coast and her winter months inland at a sheep farm in the Karoo region. It was there that Yvonne came to know the farmers who loved the earth and faced a never ending struggle for survival. Her first novel, *East to Barryvale* (Romance #1915, published in 1975), was inspired by the people of the area.

Yvonne began scribbling stories at a very early age, and in her teens she considered writing as a profession. But marriage and three daughters caused her to shelve that idea...for a while.

Then, rusty after so many years away from her writing, Yvonne enrolled in a fiction-writing course and set to work. She began with short stories and moved on to a novel, which took several months to complete. "Fortunately," she laughingly comments on her slow start, "I did not have to make a living out of my writing then. Otherwise, I would surely have starved!"

Take these
4 best-selling novels
FREE

Yes! Four sophisticated, contemporary love stories by four world-famous authors of romance FREE, as your introduction to the Harlequin Presents subscription plan. Thrill to **Anne Mather**'s passionate story BORN OUT OF LOVE, set in the Caribbean.... Travel to darkest Africa in **Violet Winspear**'s TIME OF THE TEMPTRESS....Let **Charlotte Lamb** take you to the fascinating world of London's Fleet Street in MAN'S WORLD ....Discover beautiful Greece in **Sally Wentworth**'s moving romance SAY HELLO TO YESTERDAY.

Harlequin Presents...

The very finest in romance fiction

Join the millions of avid Harlequin readers all over the world who delight in the magic of a really exciting novel. EIGHT great NEW titles published EACH MONTH! Each month you will get to know exciting, interesting, true-to-life people .... You'll be swept to distant lands you've dreamed of visiting .... Intrigue, adventure, romance, and the destiny of many lives will thrill you through each Harlequin Presents novel.

Get all the latest books before they're sold out!
As a Harlequin subscriber you actually receive your personal copies of the latest Presents novels immediately after they come off the press, so you're sure of getting all 8 each month.

Cancel your subscription whenever you wish!
You don't have to buy any minimum number of books. Whenever you decide to stop your subscription just let us know and we'll cancel all further shipments.

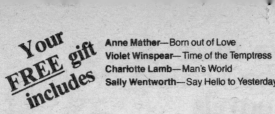